Familiar Whispers

A Paranormal Domestic Thriller

Not Safe at Home
Book 1

May Black

Previously published as **Evil Follows.**

Chapter 1
1983

Anna found herself in the kitchen and couldn't remember why. It was very late, and she should have been in bed. She held a sandwich made with the ends of the loaf. She hated the ends. Wrinkling her nose, she pulled the bread apart to reveal an orange slice of cheese. She froze when she heard Ruthie's voice.

Get out of the house.

"Why?" Anna asked.

But Ruthie didn't answer questions like that, so Anna simply obeyed. That's what she always did when Ruthie spoke. She lifted her doll from the chair, cradled her in her arm and walked, in a trance, through her home. She paused at her parents' room and peeked through the open door.

Suddenly, Anna was cold. She quickly realized she was sitting crisscross applesauce in the dirt and gravel that made up her front yard. Despite the raging fire behind her, she shivered and hugged her doll closer. Something was poking her. She reached under her leg and found the culprit. She tossed the small rock away from her.

She took a bite of her sandwich and chewed mindlessly. Rocking her doll gently back and forth, Anna watched her shadow sway and dance in front of her while behind her, her home burned to the ground, taking her parents with it.

Now, she itched. A scratchy blanket was tucked around her. A nice lady fussed over her and asked questions. Ruthie told her to be quiet, so she closed her eyes and pretended to sleep.

She didn't have to pretend for long. Anna was very tired and every muscle in her six-year-old body hurt and ached. She blocked out the sounds of firefighters and sirens and slept.

The sound of squealing brakes and crunching gravel woke her. Familiar arms lifted her, and she opened her eyes to see Aunt Lu. Lu pulled Anna onto her lap and hugged her tight. She murmured that it was all over now. She was okay. Aunt Lu was here.

Anna closed her eyes again and drifted in and out of sleep while hushed adult voices spoke.

"How old is she?"

"Six," Aunt Lu said.

"Any other children in the house?" a man's loud voice.

"No. Two adults though," Aunt Lu answered.

"We found 'em," he answered, grimly.

Another man's voice, "What's her name?"

"Anna."

"Do you know what happened?" the other voice asked. "Anna? Can she talk?"

"Honey, what happened?" Aunt Lu asked.

Anna burrowed further into her aunt's neck and shook her head. She held her doll and her sandwich, and Aunt Lu held her.

"Not now," she said.

"It's a miracle she got out," the man mumbled.

Anna drifted to sleep again, waking when she felt movement. Aunt Lu lifted her easily and propped her on her hip. She felt Aunt Lu's body move and heard the crunch of gravel beneath her boots. Anna dropped her sandwich somewhere, but she held tightly to her doll. A car door clicked open and the cinnamon scent in Aunt Lu's car told her where she was. Another set of arms held her briefly, then she was buckled into her booster seat. Aunt Jody put her arm around Anna and adjusted herself until she was comfortable.

Anna heard two thuds as car doors closed. She opened her eyes and saw Aunt Lu looking at her and Jody in the rearview mirror.

"Let's go. Now," Jody said.

Lu nodded once, and Anna felt the car start.

"You okay?" Lu asked.

Anna looked up at Aunt Jody's face. She was staring out of the window at the old tree in front of the house.

Anna felt a shiver run through Jody's body and then she felt a warm tear land on her arm. She looked up at Aunt Jody's pale face and wide eyes, still fixated on the tree.

"Jody?" Aunt Lu said as the car began to move.

Jody blinked quickly and looked down at Anna. She muttered something about being afraid of fire. Anna peeked through the window as the car pulled out. She saw heavy smoke where her home used to stand. As they drove away, she closed her eyes and once again heard Ruthie.

Safe now.

Chapter 2
1983

"Huh," Lu grunted as she hung up the phone.

"What is it?" Jody asked.

"The police want to come by and ask us some questions. And they want to talk to Anna too, as if she hasn't already been through enough," she added.

It was the day after the fire. Anna was sound asleep despite it being 11 o'clock in the morning. They knew she was exhausted and planned to let her sleep as long as she wanted.

"What's to ask? It was an accident. The idiots passed out in bed with lit cigarettes or something," Jody said. A moment passed. "I'm sorry. That was insensitive."

"I agree with you. They are, were, idiots. No, that's not why they want to come by. Apparently, Lori is missing," she said.

"What?" Jody asked. "Missing, how?"

Lu looked at her sideways.

"You know what I mean," Jody rolled her eyes. "What are they thinking? Did she run off?"

"I don't know. They didn't say on the phone. Although that explains why she's not returning our calls," Lu said.

Lori Jamieson was Anna's Child Protection Services

4

contact. She became involved with the family when Amber and David, Anna's parents, weren't sending her to school. She began home visits when Anna showed up at school with bruises on her arms and legs. Anna adored her, but Jody and Lu knew how much her parents hated Lori.

"Why do they want to talk to us about it? What would we know?" Jody asked.

Lu sighed heavily.

"They said she called the police station and wanted an officer to go to the house with her. She said she had proof that David was there. They found a note on her work calendar that said she was going to the house alone. She hasn't been seen since."

"They don't think she was in the fire?" Jody asked.

"No, I don't think so," Lu said, "This just keeps on getting better and better. They think Amber and David might have something to do with her missing."

"Wow! Like they might have hurt her or something? Were they really capable of that?" Jody knew even as she asked the question that she was grasping at straws.

Lu looked at Jody.

"Are you seriously asking if they were capable of hurting someone?"

"I know, I knew it as I said it. Of course, they were capable of that," Jody said.

"We don't know everything that went on in that house. And I can't help-," Lu stopped abruptly and glanced down the hallway where Anna still slept. She held one finger up to Jody and tiptoed to Anna's room. She peeked in. Anna was still sound asleep, curled into a tiny ball and clutching her doll. It was unlikely she would hear what Lu was about to say, but Lu wasn't taking chances. She closed the door without a sound.

"Good idea," Jody said. "She doesn't need to hear any of this yet."

Lu nodded as she sat beside Jody.

"I can't help but wonder just how bad it really was," she continued. "She says she doesn't remember what happened before she went to the hospital. And she's always said those bruises were from being clumsy and falling down or running into something. No one believes that. Why is she protecting Amber and David?"

"I don't think she's protecting them. I think she just doesn't remember. It's like she blocks out the bad stuff," Jody said.

"If that's true, what will happen when she does start to remember? Will she be able to handle it all? Will she be hurt all over again?" Lu stared at her hands as she said the last part.

"We won't know for a while. Let's not get ahead of ourselves. For now, we need to see if Anna remembers anything about Lori so we can tell the police. Then we'll deal with the memories. Anna's memories," Jody added. She long suspected Lu had her own horror stories about growing up in the same house with David. She believed Lu and Anna's childhoods were more alike than Lu wanted to admit.

"I'll talk to her first. Maybe she doesn't know anything, and she won't have to talk to the police. She's had enough trauma," Lu said.

As she stood, Jody grabbed her hand and pulled her back. She turned so she could look fully into Lu's eyes.

"If this gets too hard for you, I am here. I'll do everything I can to help you through this," she said.

Lu swiped at a tear and hugged Jody. She dried her hand on her jeans as she stood. Jody watched her walk towards Anna's room. Everyone worried about Anna, as they should. But Jody knew Lu carried her own burden. Lu knew better than anyone what David did to Anna.

Lu tapped on Anna's door and opened it slowly.

Anna was in bed under a comforter and a fluffy blanket. Her tiny body barely made a lump. She was very small for her age. Lu guessed she weighed about thirty pounds. The bones of her shoulders and back were too easy to see. They would fix that in no time.

Lu sat on the bed next to her and brushed Anna's brown hair out of her eyes. It was long and tangled across the pillow. Lu tried to comb it out with her fingers. She couldn't wait to wash it and maybe trim the ends a little. Anna had beautiful hair when someone helped her take care of it. She always left Lu and Jody's house clean and fed, only to return a few weeks later dirty and hungry. Anna's large brown eyes opened and focused on Lu. She smiled.

"Did I wake you?" Lu asked.

Anna shook her head and stretched.

"How are you feeling?"

"Happy," Anna said.

"Oh, honey," Lu murmured.

In one smooth motion, Anna threw her covers off and crawled into Lu's lap. She buried her head into Lu's shoulder. Anna still smelled like smoke from the night before, but Lu didn't care. She hugged her tight and wondered if Anna's reaction to the day before was normal. She didn't seem to realize what happened. She wasn't upset or scared. She hadn't cried and didn't even seem sad. Most kids, even abused ones, want their parents. Lu guessed she was in shock and it just hadn't hit yet. When it did, she would need all the support and love she could get.

"We need to talk," she said.

"Okay."

"Has Lori been around lately? Can you remember the last time you saw her?" Lu got straight to the point. She needed to find out if Anna knew anything before the police came.

Anna closed her eyes and shook her head once.

"I miss her," she whispered.

Lu searched her mind for words. Anna didn't answer the question, and she did that strange thing where she shook her head. It had become Anna's tell. Something she did when she wasn't being completely truthful. Anna would never admit to lying though and always promised she was telling the truth. But it looked to Lu as though she was fighting or arguing with herself.

It didn't matter now though. This wasn't the priority. Lu refused to add to Anna's trauma, but she also knew the police were worried about Lori. In fact, so was she.

Anna spoke up again, "Lori will be so happy."

"What makes you say that?" Lu asked.

"Because I'm here now. Sometimes she and Daddy would fight about it," Anna said.

Lu sat Anna up so she could see her face.

"Do you remember the last time you heard them fight?" she asked carefully.

"I don't know," Anna mumbled. She shook her head again and closed her eyes. Then she crawled from Lu's lap and scooted under her covers. As she pulled the soft blankets to her chin, Lu leaned over her and whispered.

"It's important, Anna. Please try to think for just one second. When was the last time you heard them fighting?"

"Before everything happened," Anna said through a yawn. "She didn't say goodbye to me." She closed her eyes and rolled over, pulling her doll with her.

Lu sat for another minute watching Anna drift off to sleep. Obviously, something bad had happened, and she had a strong feeling that Anna saw or heard something. And that thing she did with her head told Lu she was keeping something to herself. It might be nothing, or it might be serious. She was unlikely to figure it out though.

Lu left Anna sleeping soundly after kissing her cheek and tucking the blankets around her small frame. She needed much rest, both physically and emotionally, after the last few days.

When the police arrived, Jody let them in and led them to a seat in the den.

"Something to drink?" she asked after introductions were made.

"Yes, please," both answered as Officer Bright and Officer Paulsen made themselves comfortable.

Jody fixed tea. She was grateful to have a moment alone to collect her thoughts. Lu had told her about Anna's reaction to her questions. Jody had her own thoughts about Anna's lack of memory, but she kept them to herself.

When she entered the room, Lu was saying, "We knew they hurt Anna, so they were certainly capable of violence. Jody, let me help," Lu said as she stood to help Jody with the drinks.

Officer Bright filled Jody in on what they had been discussing, then he asked her if she could think of anything that could be helpful.

"Anything at all helps," he said, adding, "Even if you don't think it's useful, it might be."

"I know they hated Lori. She was someone in authority, and she had power. She was on to them. She knew what was going on," Jody said.

"The abuse?" Officer Paulsen asked.

"Yes. Anna always had bruises on her. Mostly her arms and thighs. Bruises that looked like fingers, like she was grabbed really hard," Lu said, demonstrating what she meant using her own arm as an example.

"And last week, I guess you know this, she ended up in the hospital," Lu paused. She couldn't bring herself to say more. "Lori was there and knew about it all."

9

"David did these things to her," Jody added.

"You are convinced it was him?" Officer Paulsen confirmed as she made a note and nodded her head encouraging them to continue.

"Yes," Lu said.

"If Lori knew about the abuse from her father, why did Anna go back there?" she asked.

"Amber, her mother, came swooping in and made a grand gesture of supposedly kicking David out and becoming the best mom ever," Lu's voice dripped of sarcasm.

"What has Anna said about it all?" Officer Paulsen asked.

Jody looked at Lu and raised her eyebrows.

"Go on," she said. "Tell them."

"Anna doesn't remember anything. She doesn't remember how she got the bruises. She doesn't remember why she was in the hospital. She doesn't remember anything at all. She explains the bruises by saying she's clumsy and bumps into things. She won't talk about the hospital or what happened leading up to it. She's never said a word to us about it, and as far as we know, she never said anything to Lori either," Lu said.

"We've wondered about brain damage. We've also wondered if she might have blocked it out, maybe an alternate personality that developed due to trauma? She also has this imaginary friend," Jody added.

She felt Lu's gaze shift abruptly to her and sensed she was close to crossing the line. She stopped talking.

Officer Paulsen seemed to pick up on the tension.

"What about the imaginary friend?"

She waited for one of them to speak.

Finally, Lu broke the silence.

"She has an imaginary friend named Ruthie. According to Anna, Ruthie talks back to her. Like Jody said, maybe she's an alternate personality. It's more than just an average kid with an imaginary friend. Ruthie is very significant in her life and appears to direct her actions and words at times. Anyway, she will be going to therapy. There's a lot to process. And to answer your original question," Lu looked at Officer Bright and caught her breath. "That is all the information we have."

"And Lori Jamieson knew all of this," Officer Bright confirmed.

Lu and Jody nodded.

"I asked Anna if she remembered anything at all about Lori being at her house. She said sometimes she would hear Lori and David fighting. Anna knew Lori wanted her to live with us, and she also knew David didn't want that," Lu said.

"Did she say when she last heard them fighting?" Officer Paulsen asked.

"She said after the hospital and 'before everything happened.' That's exactly how she said it," Lu said making air quotes.

"Does she mean they fought right before the fire?" Officer Paulsen asked.

Lu nodded in agreement, and Jody shrugged. She didn't know exactly what Anna meant, but she wasn't going to disagree with the group.

"Well, that sounds like possible motive," she said to Officer Bright.

"Agreed," he added.

"Motive? So, you really do think they did something to her?" Jody asked.

"It appears as though she decided to go to the house without waiting for an officer to escort her," Officer Bright said. "If that's the case, she was likely in danger from the Marshalls."

Lu and Jody nodded solemnly, each remembering their own violent run-ins with Amber and David.

"We will keep you informed if we discover anything," Officer Paulsen said, handing each of them a card. "And if you think of anything else, please let one of us know."

"You don't need to talk to Anna?" Lu asked, standing to walk them to the door.

"Not right now," Officer Paulsen said. "She's been through enough. What you told us confirms that Lori was at the house, and there was conflict. We really have all we need."

"Now we just need to find Lori Jamieson," Officer Bright added.

Chapter 3
1983

L u and Anna entered the office. Anna held her doll with one hand and Lu's hand with the other. As she checked in with the receptionist, Lu noticed Anna staring at a bead maze sitting in the corner.

"Go play," she said. She was certain the child had never seen a toy like that before.

Lu sat close to where Anna played and settled in for a wait. There was always a wait at the therapist's office. She watched Anna. She had that pitiful doll in a chair, propped up with plastic toy blocks on either side.

Lu studied the doll. Her pale, porcelain face was covered with a spider's web of small cracks and her kewpie mouth was pursed into a soft pink kiss. Her hair was matted flat to her head in some areas and stuck straight out in others. It was tangled and messy. Lu laughed to herself remembering the one time they tried to clean it. They painstakingly pulled at the wig and almost had it completely off. Then Anna began crying hysterically at the sight of her precious doll rendered partially bald. The wig went right back on. Anna added the small pink bow that was currently hanging on for dear life.

The doll's dress was made of an intricate lace, long, full

and fitted at the bodice. Within the folds of the bodice lurked remnants of the dress's original color, a bright, sunflower yellow. The rest of it had faded to an off white, pale yellow that reminded Lu of the inside of a banana peel.

Her left leg was damaged at the joint, so the foot was twisted in, pigeon-toed and pitiful. Her dark brown eyes were painted wide open. Unable to blink, always watching and readily returning the gaze of whoever happened to look at her. Lu avoided eye contact.

She shivered slightly and willed herself back to reality. She made a mental note to find an antique dealer. They found markings under the wig during the brief time it was off. Jody found a book on antique dolls which led them to believe the doll was made in Germany, imported and distributed in the late 1800's. But it was idle curiosity because even if it was worth something, Anna would never part with it.

Anna loved that doll. She named her Ruthie, but it occurred to Lu that Anna hadn't called the doll by name since the fire. She searched her memory and tried to think of a time in the last few days when Anna referred to Ruthie by name rather than 'my doll.'

She didn't have long to ruminate before the door opened, and Dr. Jayhala appeared. Lu stood to shake her hand. Dr. Jayhala pulled Lu to the side where they could still see Anna and asked how she was doing since their last phone call.

"The same," Lu said.

"Is she eating?" Dr. Jayhala asked.

"Yes, she's eating everything we make, and she snacks throughout the day. I guess that's a positive," she contended.

"Yes," Dr. Jayhala smiled. "How about the fire? Has she said anything about that?"

Lu didn't want Anna to hear this conversation. She shook her head and darted her eyes toward Anna.

"We can talk here," Dr. Jayhala noticed her discomfort.

"There's a white noise machine next to where she's playing. She won't be able to hear us."

Lu nodded but scooted closer to the doctor anyway.

"I'm mostly concerned about her apparent lack of interest regarding the fire," Dr. Jayhala said. "From what you told me on the phone, she doesn't seem to remember it or even realize that it happened. Has that changed since we last talked?" she asked.

Lu shook her head and sighed.

"You also told me she was abused, and she doesn't talk about that either. Or seem to remember it," the therapist said.

"She's always been like that, even when it was going on," Lu replied. Then she added, "She explained it away by saying she's clumsy."

Dr. Jayhala took a deep breath and exhaled slowly.

"I want to suggest something, but it's only a theory to be explored," she said.

"Okay," Lu looked doubtful. She was fairly certain she wasn't going to like what she was about to hear.

"Based only on our conversations, of course I haven't worked directly with Anna yet, I don't think she started the fire on purpose."

Lu held up a hand.

"She didn't start it at all. She's six," Lu's voice went up a few notches.

"Most likely not," Dr. Jayhala said quickly. "But please, let me finish. I only wonder if she did something on a subconscious level, and she is blocking it out just as she blocks out the abuse," the therapist said gently.

Lu felt tears spring into her eyes, and she brushed them away quickly. Dr. Jayhala went on.

"As I work with her, I want to see if we can get those memories back," she said.

"Why?" Lu asked. "Why make her remember such

horrible things? Isn't she happier not remembering? If she doesn't remember on her own, why force her?"

"As she grows up, those memories will likely start coming back. If she remembers bits and pieces and can't make sense of it all, that could affect her significantly, as a teenager and even into adulthood. We want her to be healthy," she added.

Lu nodded her head.

Dr. Jayhala smiled kindly.

"Please don't worry. She will be okay. She has you and Jody now, and you both are doing a beautiful job. She will be okay," Dr. Jayhala repeated.

When Lu saw Anna look at them, she waved her over. Anna stood and picked up Ruthie. She walked slowly towards the two women.

"Anna, this is Dr. Jayhala," Lu said.

Anna smiled shyly.

"Who's this?" Dr. Jayhala asked, pointing to Ruthie.

Anna hesitated.

"My doll," she said quietly.

"She's very pretty. Would you like to bring her in with you while we talk?" she asked.

Anna nodded.

Dr. Jayhala held out her hand.

"Are you ready?" she asked.

To answer, Anna took her hand and walked with her into the private office.

Lu watched them go, then she went to the play area. She busied herself tidying up where Anna was playing. She froze when she heard laughter from the next room. She shouldn't be able to hear anything from the doctor's inner office.

The white noise machine, she thought suddenly.

She looked frantically for the small box and found it, unplugged and on its side.

Anna may have heard everything.

Lu felt her body stiffen and her heart rate increase. Her stomach churned, and she stifled a burp. What exactly had they said? Anna was abused. Anna started the fire. Did she hear those things?

Lu always tended to overthink and was an expert at catastrophizing things she couldn't control. She desperately wanted to burst into the office and stop everything. She would demand to know what Anna overheard. She would take Anna home immediately and sue Dr. Jayhala.

Instead, she reflected on what she learned throughout her own years of therapy. She took deep breaths and reminded herself that it didn't help anyone when she panicked.

She tried to refocus her thoughts on the positive. Anna would be okay. She has Jody and herself to care for her. She is loved and has attention. She has her own room with a comfortable and clean bed. She has as many books and toys as she could possibly want. Overall, she was a happy little girl, and Jody and she would make sure that continued.

And she has Ruthie, Lu's inner voice added wryly.

The positive train of thought came to a screeching halt. Lu immediately thought about Ruthie again. She was certain Anna had stopped calling her by name. It used to be, "Ruthie this and Ruthie that" but now she called her "my doll." Why? Lu's mind went to PTSD next. Of course she had PTSD. How could someone go through that and not? And from there, she jumped to Dissociative Identity Disorder, convinced Ruthie was an alternate personality.

Lu was sweating now and began pacing, aware that she was failing horribly at calming herself down. She tried once again to refocus her thoughts and forced herself to think about Jody.

Jody was always the calm in the storm. Even though her unique beliefs were ultimately what brought them together, it was a topic that had faded from their lives until recently. She didn't need to say it for Lu to know what she was thinking. Jody firmly believed the house Anna and she grew up in was evil. And she figured Jody worried something had followed Anna out of the house or the doll was haunted or something like that. A promise made years earlier made Jody respect her wishes not to bring it up, but she definitely dropped some hints.

Maybe it's time to talk about that again, Lu thought. *I'd do it for Anna.*

Certain this was the distraction she needed, she asked the receptionist if there was a pay phone nearby. Before she answered, Anna and Dr. Jayhala came out and Lu told her never mind. Anna was smiling, but the therapist wasn't.

Anna quickly hugged Lu and then ran back to the bead maze. Lu moved to where Dr. Jayhala was waiting.

"Still nothing," she said. "Let's schedule for next week, and I'll continue to work with her on those memories."

"Your white noise machine is off," Lu hissed. "She probably heard us earlier."

Dr. Jayhala looked to the corner where the machine usually sat. She shook her head slowly.

"No, I doubt it," she said, still shaking her head. She mindlessly rubbed her furrowed brow.

"Did she say anything about hearing what we said?" Lu asked again.

"No, but even if she did hear us, isn't it a good thing? For her to know what happened to her?" she asked.

For the second time that day Lu felt her blood pressure increasing and her stomach knotting. No, this isn't what she wanted after all. She wanted Anna to be healthy but not if it meant pulling horrible memories from her tiny mind.

"No," Lu said through clenched teeth. "It's not a good thing. Not now anyway. If she ever asks, I will tell her. In my way."

Lu was surprised by the ferocity of her words. An overwhelming desire to protect Anna burned in her chest.

"Why not now?" the therapist asked softly. She was still looking at the corner where the white noise machine should have been humming.

"The truth is too hard. She's better off never knowing. We're leaving now," she announced. "Anna, come on."

"Are we coming back?" Anna asked. She straightened the toy area quickly and picked up her doll. She smoothed the dress and checked the bow.

"I hope so," Dr. Jayhala affirmed.

At the same time, Lu said, "No."

As she drove home, Lu thought about what she would tell Jody. Jody deserved to know what happened, but Lu was almost certain she would take it as an opportunity to drop hints about her own theories again. While talking to Jody about that had seemed like a good idea earlier, she was having second thoughts now.

She justified her change of mind by telling herself that she wasn't thinking clearly. Her own memories, combined with her fears for Anna, were the only reasons she briefly entertained Jody's theories. Now that she was thinking straight, Lu was confident that she didn't want to explore all that nonsense again.

Chapter 4
1977

J ody returned to the house she shared with her older sister, Lynda. She barely got out of the car before Lynda was hobbling down the walkway, trying to manage a pair of crutches while keeping her foot from touching the ground.

"What are you doing?" she asked. "Get back in the house and rest. I'll tell you everything in a second."

Lynda pouted but obeyed as she swung the crutches around and hobbled back to her spot on the couch.

"So?" Lynda questioned once they both were settled, and her foot was propped up on a pillow.

Jody just shook her head.

"They ran me off," she said. "I can't believe it, but they actually had a shotgun and they ran me off. Told me to 'git off their land,' if you can imagine it."

"Wow," Lynda said. "Are you okay?"

"Yes, just creeped out. I mean, Lynda, the house. Oh my gosh. And that tree in the front yard. I swear I could see a body hanging from it. Like, this wispy figure. Probably just the dust from the place messing with my eyes," she concluded.

"Maybe," Lynda said.

Jody knew what she was thinking. They both saw strange

things often. The only difference was that Lynda tried to talk to the strange things and Jody pretended they weren't there. Jody wasn't scared. She just preferred it when wispy spirits weren't hanging around her, literally or figuratively.

Jody and Lynda had a unique hobby. They inherited a fascination with all things spiritual and historical from a long line of ancestors who avidly gathered information. Lynda was an empath, just as their mother and grandmother were.

Jody, however, was more interested in history and knowing the stories behind the spirits. While she was also an empath, she wasn't interested in honing her skills beyond what she was naturally born with. Their oldest sister, May, had no interest at all in any of the family's gifts. She left home years ago, only visiting during holidays.

It was that way even as children. Whenever their mother, Greta, channeled spirits and spoke in those strange voices, Lynda was rapt with attention. Jody stayed, but she really wanted to leave the room. May left.

Their grandmother called it their special gift. She liked to remind them that, if people had known about their gift a hundred years ago, they would have been burned as witches and the three girls would never have existed.

Greta wasn't as dramatic. She simply taught her daughters their craft and watched closely as they grew. Through the years, Lynda became more and more like their mother and eventually learned how to channel spirits.

That's why she was always the one out there talking to people, while Jody hung back with her nose in a book. The fall that resulted in Lynda's broken foot also resulted in bed rest for a nasty bump on the head. She couldn't travel and had to trust her sister to handle her part of the job. Jody promised to come back with all the details if Lynda promised to stay quiet and rest. She knew what she asked was hard for Lynda.

Especially considering what the sisters recently learned. Their family was connected to a house in town that was supposed to be haunted. Jody researched the old home and was convinced their own ancestors had something to do with the house and the family who lived there. She was ready to send Lynda with the information she had gathered when the accident happened. Now she enjoyed teasing Lynda by stalling.

"Come on, Jody. Tell me what happened. Who was hanging from the tree? I know you saw something," Lynda said. She absentmindedly scratched her leg just inside the top of her cast.

"Start at the beginning and tell me what happened," Lynda insisted.

"Well it's pretty run down. Even though it's old, it could be restored. But once I saw the people living there, there's no way. I think there are four adults there, and I heard a baby crying," she said.

"Really? There's a baby? Whose is it?" Lynda questioned.

"The brother's girlfriend. His name is David and her name is..." Jody flipped through the notes she made in the car after leaving the house. "Here it is. The girlfriend is Amber, and the baby's name is Anna. I didn't actually see her, but the grandmother fussed at Amber to quiet Anna. So, I'm assuming that's the baby's name."

"Okay, go on," Lynda urged.

Jody told Lynda how she knocked on the door for a few minutes before a man answered. It turned out to be David, the adult son who lived there now. Once she bribed him with a twenty-dollar bill, he let her in for a brief conversation. They were talking about the house, basic history, age, who built it and when, when the grandfather appeared, and David abruptly stopped talking.

"This tiny old man appeared and the young, stronger one regressed to a child. He acted like he was afraid of getting into trouble," she said.

"And he was just talking about the history of the house, right?"

"Yup," Jody replied. "Then I pushed my luck," she added with a sideways smile.

"Tell me," Lynda implored.

When the old man appeared and Jody saw the change in demeanor, she knew she'd found the person to answer her questions about the house and the rumors of hauntings and spirits living there. The old man could barely walk, and David immediately helped him to a couch. He seemed to sink into it and looked even smaller, more frail, than he did before.

"David told him who I was and that I had questions about the house's history," she said. "I asked him if he'd always lived there, and he said 'yes.' Then I asked him if he ever experienced anything unusual. Like things moving on their own, strange sounds, or even seen anything strange."

She told Lynda about the look on the old man's face as she asked these questions. His eyes bugged out of his head, and he started to turn red in the face. He worked his thin lips around the few teeth he had left, and his shaggy eyebrows danced up and down on his forehead.

"I assumed he was either getting excited or getting mad. David was pacing the room and, before the grandfather could speak, Amber walked in with the grandmother. That's when the baby started crying, and she ordered Amber to go shut Anna up. That's what she said, Lynda, to a new mother. So sad."

"Wow," Lynda said, shaking her head slowly. "Did the grandfather manage to tell you anything?"

Jody explained that he never had a chance because the grandmother went into overdrive. She started yelling at Jody to leave the house. And she threatened her.

"That's when she got the shotgun and told me to 'git off her land'! She could barely lift the thing, and David tried to help her. She got really angry with him and when she finally got it raised to her shoulder, she aimed it at David."

Lynda covered her mouth with both hands. Her blood ran cold hearing that her sister was so close to being injured.

"Oh no! Jody, are you all right? I'm so sorry," she began to move towards her sister for a comforting hug, but Jody stopped her.

"What?" she asked, annoyed and confused.

"This is the part you're going to love. When she got the shotgun up to her shoulder, the grandfather started having a coughing fit. She and David went to him, and it's like I wasn't even there. I stood back for a while and watched them as they fussed over him, and while I was doing that..." she let her words trail off in an enticing way.

Lynda had enough. "Tell me already!" she cried.

"I saw it Lynda," she whispered. "I saw the spirit who haunts the house. It was a young boy, maybe a teenager. He wore old tattered clothes. He had a rope around his neck," she described.

Lynda rubbed the goosebumps on her arms.

"That had to be...challenging for you," Lynda said.

"You don't have to worry," Jody replied. "You're still the ghost hunter in the family. I don't want your job."

She remembered the day Lynda became the one who really mattered. Their mother, Greta, passed away in a car accident leaving all three daughters lost and confused. Then, one evening, Lynda calmly told Jody and May something that changed everything.

"Mom is here. She's with us, and she's talking to me," Lynda had said.

That was the turning point when their talents truly took different paths. Lynda could sense things and talk to spirits, including their mother. She had the gift. The real and true gift, not what Jody had, which was mostly just a feeling. May thought them foolish and wanted nothing to do with any of it.

Jody was jealous at first, but when she really was honest with herself, she was perfectly happy to dig around in archives and flip through microfiche until her eyes crossed. She found obscure books about history and talked to people for firsthand accounts whenever she could. She knew she was valuable to the team and pretended that it didn't matter to her that Mom spoke to Lynda and not her.

"I know. That's not what I meant," Lynda said. "Just tell me what happened next?"

"Well, I left," she said.

"What! Why?" Lynda asked.

"I guess because this is where it became 'challenging' for me," Jody said, making air quotes.

Lynda rolled her eyes.

Jody ignored her and continued. "He looked at me. The spirit looked directly at me and pointed at me. I've never felt anything like that before, and I don't want to again. It was scary," she admitted.

Lynda scooted closer to her sister and pulled her into a hug.

"I'm okay," Jody kept saying as Lynda held her tight.

Finally, she pulled back and looked Jody in the eye. "Are you sure?" she asked.

"Yes, it was shocking but also kind of exciting. I'm even more curious to find the connection between our families. It was like he knew who I was," she added.

"The spirit?" Lynda asked.

"Yes. He showed up when everyone else was busy with the grandfather. He stood where they couldn't see him, and he looked only at me. That was the most alarming thing about it all. Not that he appeared, more that he seemed to really notice me," Jody said.

Lynda nodded along agreeing with everything Jody had said. Finally, she asked, "So you left?"

"I just walked out of the house. I'm not even sure the family saw me leave. I just got in the car, drove a little ways away, stopped to make notes and then drove here. I'll happily let you handle the interactions with that house from now on," Jody insisted.

Jody could tell Lynda was itching to go to the house herself, and Jody was fine with that arrangement. She wouldn't fully admit it to her sister, but she was certain she would never forget the feeling of terror she experienced when the boy pointed at her. While Lynda was even more excited, Jody was filled with foreboding and even fear.

"Wish me luck," Jody cried as she pulled out of the driveway.

Lynda waved as her sister drove down the street.

Since her experience at the house, Jody happily moved back into her role of historian. She would deal with the flesh and blood, living people and let Lynda handle the ghostly ones.

She enjoyed the hour and a half drive to Knoxville and studied a map to find the house where Louise Marshall lived. Louise was David's younger sister. She left for college a few years ago and was currently living a hundred miles away. After several phone calls and messages, Louise had reluctantly agreed to meet with her. Jody explained that she was doing research on old homes in upper East Tennessee and the Marshall home in Jonesboro was the one she was most interested in.

Despite Louise's protests that she knew next to nothing about the house, Jody convinced her that any information at all would be helpful.

When she pulled into the Fort Sanders area, she drove in aimless circles. A maze of one-way roads made it almost impossible to reach the house. At one point, she could see the house, and after checking the map, was convinced she would finally reach it. She sped up and then slammed on her brakes after turning a corner. A construction crew blocked the entire road.

She began another circuit around Fort Sanders, fondly called The Fort by those who lived there. As she drove, she tried to picture the area during the Civil War in 1863. The Fort was occupied by Union forces who were welcomed by mostly pro-Union counties in the area. Knoxville was important to both armies because of the direct railroad route that would carry supplies and information for the winner.

It was hard to picture grassy hills and dirt piles where old houses, small stores, and restaurants now stood. She turned right onto Seventeenth Street. One wall of The Fort ran parallel to this street. She passed Laurel which, along with Clinch Street, was where the front of The Fort stood. Jody thought she could hear the cries of Confederate soldiers entangled in telegraph wire laid as a trap around Fort Sanders. She shuddered as she rolled her window up and turned on the radio.

Finally, construction cleared, and she managed to reach the back of the house. She didn't care that she had to walk around to the front. She was just grateful to find parking on the road and finally get out of the car. Most of the houses in the area were old and somewhat run down. They lived long lives being inhabited by partying college students and maintained by persistent contractors who had an endless supply of materials to patch any problem.

Even though she wasn't the talented empath in the family, she clearly felt the presence of Civil War soldiers all around her. Over eight hundred had died there. Many were trapped in the ditch that ran around Fort Sanders while Union sharpshooters took their shots.

Jody sensed other deaths too. She wasn't surprised. Any time an old area was restored and lived in, the spirits never seemed to rest. Based on the thumping sound of music coming from the house next door, she doubted the living were able to rest either.

The door opened before she knocked and a young woman about her age appeared. She had short brown hair, cut strategically so it was easy for Jody to count at least seven piercings in her ears. Her large, brownish green eyes crinkled as she smiled at Jody. She wore cut off jean shorts and a bright orange University of Tennessee shirt.

"Come in," she said. Jody followed her through the door and caught a whiff of cinnamon scented incense.

"Louise?" Jody asked.

"Call me Lu," she said. "Jody, right?"

Jody nodded.

"Come to the kitchen," Lu said. Her bare feet padded across the floor as she led Jody to a chair that sat facing what passed for a garden along the side of the house.

"A drink? Water, Coke, beer?" she asked as she rummaged through the refrigerator.

"Coke would be great," Jody answered. She leaned back in the chair and made herself comfortable. She was relieved to be so welcomed here especially after the reception she received at the Marshall's house. She kicked off her wedges and pulled her long hair into a ponytail. It was hot in the small kitchen. She pulled a notebook from her bag and dug deeper for a pen.

When she looked up again, Lu was adjusting a box fan so that it blew cool air directly on her. The drinks were on the table, already sweating. Lu sat opposite her and smiled.

They both laughed comfortably and settled into a casual conversation. They talked about their age. Both in their early twenties. They talked about their interests. Both in college studying psychology. They talked about their dating life. Both single. Then they moved on to the reason for Jody's visit.

"I went to your home in Jonesboro the other day," Jody began tentatively.

"Did they try to shoot you," Lu asked, laughing.

"Kind of," Jody said.

Lu stopped laughing immediately. "You're kidding. Oh my gosh, I am so sorry."

This time Jody laughed.

"It was your grandmother, I think. She didn't seem to like me very much. I also met your brother, David. I didn't feel threatened. It's cool."

Lu nodded thoughtfully.

"My parents died when David and I were young. A car accident. We were raised by our grandparents who are definitely out of touch. Very set in their backwards, country ways. That shotgun comes out more often than I like," she added dryly.

Jody nodded along with Lu. "I also lost my mother to a car accident not long ago," she said.

The women sat silently for a moment, each lost in thought about their losses. Then Lu took a long sip of her Coke and leaned back in her chair.

"So, you have some questions about the house? I'm not sure what I can tell you that you couldn't just look up. It's really old. Lots of history apparently," she related.

"My questions are more about the people who lived there over the years. Your family," Jody paused when Lu's face fell. Her smile disappeared.

"I can't help you with that," she said abruptly. She stood and picked up her glass. Dumping the remains in the sink, she turned back to Jody.

"Sorry," she continued. "I guess you wasted your time."

Lu stood expectantly, waiting for Jody to stand up. Jody stayed seated and avoided eye contact.

"Let me start over," she said. She searched her mind for the right words to use. Obviously asking about her family wasn't the way to go. Jody fell back on the familiar and decided to focus on the history of the house. Just the facts.

"I think the house was built in the late 1800s. Do you

happen to know the exact date?" she queried, still avoiding eye contact.

Lu sighed.

"You want to know if the house is haunted," she said as she sat back down.

Jody opened her mouth to protest but shut it when Lu kept speaking.

"No, don't say anything. I know that's what you want to know. You are too polite to come right out and say it that way, but I know that's what you want. Is the house haunted? Have I seen a ghost? Who haunts the house? Is it evil? And maybe, why is my family so weird? Am I right?" Lu waited for an answer.

"Yes. I would never have put it that way though. I would hope I was more sensitive than that," she finally looked Lu in the eye. "But look, I don't want to make you uncomfortable. You don't have to tell me anything you're not okay with."

"Nah, it's cool. Let's talk over dinner tonight. You can crash here if you want. My other roommate is gone for the weekend. You can have her room," Lu said.

Jody smiled and nodded.

"I would love that," she said.

"Great! I'll cook, we'll get some wine, and I promise I will tell you everything I know about the house. And then we never have to talk about it again, okay?" Lu said.

Jody's heart leapt when Lu insinuated that there would be other opportunities for them to talk about it.

That night over dinner, Lu told Jody about the rumors that her house was haunted and evil. She never had friends growing up because no one wanted their precious child around those weird Marshalls. She told her how it was so bad, even stories of the house being haunted were overshadowed by the illegal things her family did. They were always in trouble with the police. She talked about that stupid shotgun and how quick they were to grab it anytime they felt inconvenienced.

She told her about the rumors of a curse on the family and the terrible things that happened in the house. She told her almost everything about growing up in the house. Jody didn't take notes. She intended to keep her promise to never bring it up again.

"What do you mean you promised her you wouldn't talk about it again? So you're just giving up?" Lynda was mindlessly moving folders and stacks of paper from one place to another.

Jody watched and waited. Finally, Lynda slammed the last stack of paper onto her desk. Breathing hard, she took a deep breath and looked at Jody.

"I thought we were doing this together," she said.

"We can still work together. I'm not giving up on you," she said gently. "I'm just not going any further into that particular house."

"Because you made a promise to our subject," Lynda said.

Jody took a deep breath. Lynda knew how to push her buttons no matter how hard she tried to ignore it. She counted to ten in her mind and took deep cleansing breaths. Then, she exploded.

"Her name is Lu, not 'subject.' You are such a hypocrite. It's okay for you to have a boyfriend, but as soon as I get interested in someone, suddenly I'm abandoning you, and I'm giving up, and I'm a terrible sister. You're so pitiful," she flopped into a nearby chair and glared at her sister. What little patience she had was gone.

The sisters stared at each other for several moments, each trying to read the other's thoughts. Jody knew Lynda was about to accuse her of being jealous of her ability to talk to Greta.

"It's not that," she said before Lynda could speak. It was an old routine that played out each time they fought.

"I know," Lynda placated. "I know."

The sisters continued to glare at each other.

"I care about her," Jody said. "I think we could have something. And she asked me to stop. It bothers her, Lynda. Can't you understand that? There's something strange there, and it really bothers her. I want to respect that. What am I supposed to do?"

"You're right. I get it," Lynda said. "If it means we stop looking into the Marshall house and our connection to it, then that's what we do. Your happiness is more important. If Lu makes you happy, you should do whatever you have to do to be with her."

"So you'll stop, too?" Jody asked.

"Yes. Although I can't believe you didn't even tell her. She might actually find it interesting that our families are connected through the house. I'll bet it's a cool story," Lynda said.

"Maybe. But it's just not worth it. Thank you for understanding," Jody said.

She smiled as she hugged her sister, but then her heart skipped when Lynda uttered a single phrase.

"Mom says it won't matter anyway."

Chapter 5
2019

Anna sat in an overstuffed chair with her short legs curled under her. She looked around the office and took in the homey and relaxing decor. The soft browns and dark pinks were her favorite color scheme. She sighed thinking about the amount of time she spent in therapy, and she felt like she never made any progress. She still didn't remember her childhood and lived under a nagging guilt that she had started the fire that killed her parents. Even though no one had ever come right out and said that to her, she managed to pick up enough through the years to know it was possible.

"How are you feeling?" Dr. Rhodes asked. She was settling into a chair across from Anna with a stack of notebooks and her fancy pen.

"Frustrated and irritated," Anna replied.

"About what?" she asked as she opened a fresh notebook.

"Well, for one thing, the number of notebooks it takes to figure me out," she said, eyeing the stack at the doctor's feet.

Dr. Rhodes chuckled softly.

"It's more about how I like to take notes than anything. I write big, too," she added, flashing an open page full of her scribbles. "What's on your mind?"

"It's these dreams I keep having. I'm fighting someone or something, and I'm always in that house. And then I wake up and I'm so out of sorts. I can't focus on anything. I'm almost itchy. Like I can't stand being in my skin. Lily says I'm grumpy," Anna said.

Dr. Rhodes smiled. Anna hadn't introduced her to her daughter Lily, but she showed her plenty of pictures. Dr. Rhodes counseled her through the postpartum depression that followed Lily's birth. In the six years since, Dr. Rhodes had seen most every picture she had saved on her phone.

"Poor Lily," she smiled.

Anna laughed too.

"How are things at work?" Dr. Rhodes asked.

"Same. That frustrates and irritates me too. Nothing I do is ever enough. I have too many kids on my caseload to have the time, much less the energy, to do what's really needed for each one. There're not enough teachers. We are all overloaded. And administration acts like that isn't a problem. Of course, if we bring it up, then something must be wrong with us," she said.

Dr. Rhodes nodded, and Anna continued.

"Abhay says I have too much work stress. The Aunts agree with him. Of course, they would. And I do see why. So many of my students struggle, and it breaks my heart at the end of every school day. You can tell some of them don't want to go home. There's this one little girl...Child Protective Services came to the school to talk to her. I guess it reminded me of Lori," Anna said.

"Lori was your CPS worker, right?"

Anna nodded.

"If I remember correctly, you never heard from her again after the fire."

Anna nodded again.

"She is definitely tied to that very traumatic time of your childhood. It makes sense that seeing this little girl, and CPS, would stir things up for you. Sounds like you experienced a trigger," Dr. Rhodes suggested. "Anything else?"

Anna knew this was her chance to tell Dr. Rhodes about hearing Ruthie. Anna had freely talked about her interactions with Ruthie when she was a child, referring to her as an imaginary friend. She even admitted Ruthie was her doll's name. But she always left out the small detail that Ruthie still talked to her and in fact, had never stopped talking to her. For the last thirty years, Anna told no one that Ruthie was still with her.

"No, that's it. I guess," she mumbled.

"We talk a lot about after the fire, when you lived with your aunts. We don't talk much about what life was like for you before the fire. I suspect that's a big part of the dreams. Your subconscious is trying to tell you something. What do you think?" she asked.

"You know I don't remember much of anything. I have these large blocks of time where I just can't remember anything concrete. I can't picture anything going on. Like holidays. Shouldn't I be able to remember them?"

"I think it would be a good idea to revisit those blocked memories again. I know it hasn't gone well the last few times we've tried, but you are older now and more self-aware. Each year that passes, you change. Maybe this is the time to dig deep again," Dr. Rhodes proposed.

She sat back in her chair and allowed Anna to process what she'd just said.

"I guess so," Anna began. "I want to remember, and I try so hard to. But it's like a brick wall that I can't see over or around. It just stands there, stopping me from remembering. Stopping me from everything."

She let her words hang in the air, suspecting it was Ruthie who blocked her memories but unable to explain how. She couldn't explain something she didn't understand.

"How's your journaling going?" Dr. Rhodes asked.

This was another touchy subject. Anna knew writing made her feel better and helped her process emotions. She would do great for weeks at time, journaling every single day. But, as soon as she got close to discovering something new, her mind would freeze, and she would stop writing. There was nothing to say, nothing to write.

"Not today," Anna said. "I just can't."

"Okay. Then why don't we focus on the dreams and the house. Relax and let your mind wander. Tell me everything you can about the house in your dreams. Is it the same as the actual house? What do you remember?" Dr. Rhodes asked.

She dug through her notebooks and pulled out one that held Anna's childhood memories. It was a thin notebook.

Anna thought back to what she learned over the years. It was a very old house and had been in her family for generations. Marshalls had always lived there and many of them died there.

There were stories that the house was haunted. There were even rumors that the house was cursed. In fact, so many people were curious about it and the stories around it, that historians and ghost hunters alike contacted them often. Her parents eventually painted a "keep out" sign on the front porch. They didn't like visitors.

She smiled.

"You know that's how my aunts met. Because of the house," she remarked.

Dr. Rhodes nodded as Anna recounted the familiar story. Aunt Jody and her sister were investigating their house, drawn there by rumors of a haunting. She visited the house one day, but no one would talk to her. The story goes, Lu's grandmother ran Jody off with a shotgun. Luckily, Jody found Aunt Lu taking classes at the University of Tennessee. They grew closer and eventually married.

"That's a great story," Dr. Rhodes said. "They did an

amazing job raising you. But back to the house itself. Anything?"

Anna experienced a few strange events while growing up. She remembered them easily despite Lu's increasing reluctance to talk about them. Lu's childhood bedroom became Anna's, and they each experienced common happenings when they lived there. They didn't talk about them though. Not anymore.

"Yes, it's the same house in my dreams. And some of the same things happen in my dreams that also happened in real life," Anna answered.

"Like what?"

"Things would get broken. I always got in trouble for it, but it was never me," she mused.

"How did you get in trouble?"

"Yelled at. A lot," Anna mumbled.

"What kinds of things were broken?" Dr. Rhodes asked.

"Glasses, especially if they were full, so they spilled everywhere. Sometimes ashtrays would end up on the floor. And things in the kitchen would be moved around or knocked into the sink or on the floor. It's like we had a pesky cat that liked to play with things. But we didn't," Anna said.

"Go on," Dr. Rhodes prompted.

"The history is very sketchy. At least, what I know of it. I've always heard some of my ancestors died in the house which makes sense. Back in the day, that's what happened. It's not like there were hospitals to go to. There's one story that is so creepy. A man, one of my ancestors, was killed by people in the town. He was hung in front of the house. Sometimes, in my dreams, I feel his presence. I think it's him anyway. He's angry and mean. And sometimes, he looks like my father," she added quietly.

Dr. Rhodes made a note in her notebook. While she scribbled, she prodded for more details. "Anything else?"

"I know what you're getting at. No, I don't have any new

memories of Ruthie. Sometimes she's in my dreams but not always. If she does show up, she's telling me to run or hide or just go away. And nothing ever about the fire or how it started or even what was going on before it," she said.

"That's not exactly what I was getting at, but it is interesting. Do you think there is some part of your mind that Ruthie represents? A part that doesn't want you to remember?" Dr. Rhodes asked.

Anna thought for several seconds. It wasn't like that. It was more a feeling deep within. A paralyzing fear that exposing her heart, exposing the memories, would somehow end her. She couldn't say that though. She didn't even want to hear those words come from her own mouth.

"I'm not sure," she finally said. She knew she was avoiding the real issues, as usual.

"Last time we talked about Ruthie, you said that other than the dreams, you hadn't heard her in your mind since you were a little girl." Dr. Rhodes flipped through another notebook.

"I'm wondering about the triggers at work and with the dreams starting again. Do you hear her now?"

Anna looked down. She was ready to talk about this. She wanted to clear the air and blurt out the words that choked her every time. She worked her mouth, preparing it to say the words she dreaded so intensely. She wanted to be honest and do the work to free her mind and her spirit from the dead weight she had been dragging around for the last thirty years. She was ready to stop running. Ready to find out how her parents died in the fire while she sat unharmed in the front yard with no memory of the night at all. She screwed up her courage, heart beating fast, sweat beads forming on her forehead, hands clenched.

"No, I don't hear from her. Not since the fire," she said.

Yet, even as she spoke those words to Dr. Rhodes, in her mind she heard, *Run*, over and over again.

"Run? From what?" Abhay asked for the fourth time in the last hour.

Anna closed her eyes. Maybe she shouldn't have told him she heard Ruthie. She had come very close to telling Dr. Rhodes and had been conflicted the entire drive home. It didn't help that when she got there, he was waiting for her with a glass of wine, ready to give her his full attention.

Abhay was the love of her life. He knew everything about her and had experienced much of it alongside her. His mother, May, was Jody's sister and, while the sisters weren't very close, Jody and her nephew had a strong connection. Abhay visited frequently when Anna lived with Jody and Lu after the fire. They easily became fast friends and virtually inseparable. Then they became teenagers and their friendship blossomed into a long courtship, and eventually, they married. Now they were married almost sixteen years and had a daughter of their own.

Despite his young age at the time, Abhay was there for her after the fire. He provided a comfort and compassion for Anna that she grew to rely on throughout the years. When she couldn't find the words to talk to anyone else, she always found the words with him. And he always waited patiently until she did. That's why she finally broke down and told him she was hearing Ruthie. He was the only one she could tell. And he already knew something was going on with her. She couldn't hide it any longer.

He reacted just like she knew he would. Strong and brave by her side, but still worried and feeling helpless. And he was getting on her nerves. He had to stop asking that question.

"Again, I don't know. I wish I did," she answered, eyes still closed.

She felt his hand on hers, and their fingers instinctively entwined. She looked down at her pale fingers alternating with

39

his light brown ones. It made her smile, and she immediately relaxed. She laid her head back and closed her eyes again.

"It's okay," he finally said. "We'll figure it out."

Anna nodded and wiped away a tear. He was so understanding and supportive. Sometimes, that only made it worse.

"Did Dr. Rhodes have any thoughts?" he asked.

"No, not really. Of course, I didn't tell her either," Anna opened one eye carefully and looked at Abhay.

He made a face at her and sighed.

"I know, I know. I'll tell her next time. It's not like it's easy to just say, 'Oh, by the way, I hear voices in my head.' Give me some time," Anna half joked.

Abhay smiled. "Okay, I get it. What about the dreams? Does she have any ideas about that?"

"Nothing beyond what you already said about work being stressful. And, of course, CPS being there for Camilla was a sort of trigger," she said. She sat still with her eyes closed and her head resting on the back of the couch.

"Anything else? Do you want to talk some more?" Abhay asked.

Anna shook her head slowly. She just wanted to sit quietly for a bit.

"Okay, then. I'm going to get our girl from Jessie's. Want me to pick up anything for dinner while I'm out?" he asked. He bent over Anna and kissed her cheek.

"No, I'll make something," Anna said. She enjoyed cooking. It was a comforting hobby and would distract her. "And I'm going to call The Aunts and invite them next weekend. Have them stay the night. Okay?"

"Do it!" Abhay said. "They need to see their great niece. It's been a while. Lily will be thrilled. And it will help you too, I think."

When he closed the door, Anna stood and stretched. Her Aunt Lu and Abhay's Aunt Jody made an unusual little family, especially when Anna joined them after her parents died. She and Abhay were unusually close to their aunts. They often referred to them as 'The Aunts.' A term of endearment that didn't come close to how they both felt about them.

As she prepared spaghetti and salad, Anna thought about Aunt Lu and the memories they shared. Anna knew that despite her trepidation, Lu had tried several times through the years to help Anna remember her childhood. But it was always the same story. Anna didn't remember then, and she didn't remember now. And Lu wasn't telling her anything she couldn't remember on her own. Lu didn't want to talk about the past if she could avoid it. Anna thought she had made peace with not knowing and even started saying that she didn't really want to know. She made the decision to focus on the present and what was going on in her life now.

Despite her determination that all was fine, and she didn't need answers, deep down she always knew that was a lie. She never could stop her mind from wandering to the past, and she often thought about the times she clearly heard Ruthie as a child. While so many memories were locked away, others came to her easily. Like making up stories to explain away her bruises. She couldn't just say she didn't remember how she got them. Her teachers wanted to know what happened. So did Lori. In fact, Lori asked a lot of questions.

Chapter 6
1983

The lady was barely out of the car before Mama was yelling down the drive. Anna watched from one of the coolest spots on the first floor. All the windows were open, so she could hear every word clearly and still stay hidden.

"Who the hell are you?" Mama squinted and held her hand up to block the sun from her eyes. She didn't see daylight too often.

"I'm Lori Jamieson, Mrs. Marshall. It's nice to meet you," the lady said, and she held out her hand to shake as she walked up the dirt path to the porch.

Mama just stared at her, and the lady dropped her hand and stopped at the bottom step. Mama was huffing and puffing from having to get up and move to the door. It was hot and humid today. Even though it was fall, the temperatures still swung wildly from hot to cold.

This day though was hot, and there was no breeze and no reason to think tomorrow would be any better. They had one fan, but it wasn't running, and earlier Daddy told her not to open the fridge door because she might let the cold air out. He said this while holding the door wide open looking for a beer.

She could also see that Mama had her legs spread funny,

trying to stand on the strongest boards so she wouldn't go crashing through the porch. Anna kind of hoped that would happen. It would be very funny, especially since she was trying so hard to look scary. The lady stood on the very bottom step and looked up. She ignored the white thigh skin poking through Mama's sweatpants, even though she must have had a pretty good view.

Anna listened with growing excitement as the lady told Mama that she had to send Anna to school now. She was six years old, and school had started in August. Thankfully someone had reported it, so they were able to help Mama and Daddy get her in school.

Mama wanted to know why it was such a big deal. Why can't she wait until next year? The lady explained it was the law, and she used fancy words Anna didn't really know the meaning of. She wasn't too sure Mama knew the meaning either. She kept saying 'true ants see.' Anna couldn't figure out what school had to do with ants seeing.

Mama said something about homeschooling, and Anna's heart froze. No, no no! She most definitely did not want Mama teaching her anything. Anna was young, but she knew enough to know this was not a good idea.

Mama was getting louder and louder. Anna watched the lady walk backward to her car. She was smart not to turn her back on Mama. The lady said Mama had to get Anna to school Monday. She said she would come back with the police if she didn't. Anna knew her parents did not like the police. They were always talking about hiding things from them because the cops could come and take their stuff if they didn't. Anna wondered if she was one of the things they hid.

The lady closed her car door, and Mama started screaming for Daddy. Anna stayed where she was. She could still hear everything, and if she had to make a break for it, she could always jump out the open window. She listened to her parents.

Mama told Daddy what the lady said, that they had to

send Anna to school, or the cops would come. They got louder and louder as they got each other worked up. They shouted and cussed, hollered and threatened. They were angry about having to send Anna to school and how much money that was going to cost them. They questioned whose business was it anyway? They reminded each other that they could do whatever they wanted, damn the law. The liquor bottle came out. Anna took her cue and quietly made her way to her bedroom while she still had a chance.

Anna loved to read and had a treasury of books hidden in the back of her closet. Aunt Lu gave them all to her, but it was a secret. She sat on the floor thinking about which book to choose and absentmindedly ran her finger down the familiar scratch marks on the walls and the inside of the door. Last year, she got the courage to ask Mama why they were there. Did an animal get caught or something? Mama said to ask Daddy. It was his family's house, so the curse was his problem. When she asked Daddy, he just said something about it being a long time ago and don't be talking about things like that.

Anna stopped talking about them, but she kept on wondering about them. Especially at night when she could swear she heard something in there scratching at the wood. She learned that if she kept the door open at night, she wouldn't hear the scratching. She kept it closed during the day though, just in case someone climbed the stairs and found the books and other treasures she stored there.

She ran her finger down the longest scratch before choosing a book and closing the door. The argument and yelling downstairs had escalated to throwing things. Anna heard something shatter and wondered which dish was broken now. Eventually they would run out of dishes to eat off of. Things were always being broken around their home.

The shouting and throwing happened a lot, and she learned early on to keep out of sight and out of sound. Eventually one of them would leave, and the other one would keep drinking or would take their medicine to calm down. Then, after a while, the other one would come back and take their medicine too, and they would both sleep for a day, sometimes two. When they woke up, they would be hungry but not mad anymore.

It used to scare her when they would sleep so much, but over time, it became her favorite time. It was quiet in the house, and she could move around as much as she wanted. Aunt Lu and Aunt Jody gave her their phone number and said she could call them any time if she needed something. Mostly she didn't need anything. The peace and quiet was enough for her.

Chapter 7
1983

Anna loved school. Even though she started a little late, she was still smarter than most of the other kids. She could read better, and she could write too. And she had a secret. The lady who visited her house that day also visited her at school. Anna was pretty sure Mama and Daddy didn't know this, and she sure wasn't going to tell them. She loved seeing Lori there.

The only bad thing about school was all the questions. Anna didn't know how to answer them, but at least she had Ruthie to help.

"Those bruises have to hurt," Ms. Canter said. "Did you fall down? Why don't you go see Nurse Janey? Maybe she can give you an ice pack or something."

Anna took the pink nurse's slip and left her kindergarten classroom. She walked slowly down the hall. With Ruthie's help, she formed answers to the questions she knew she would be asked. Nurse Janey never missed anything, so Anna had to be ready.

Last time Nurse Janey looked at Anna's bruises, she put her own hands on Anna and made her fingers match up with the bruise marks. She told Anna it looked like someone grabbed her arm and made the marks.

"What happened?" she asked.

Anna loved Nurse Janey. She was so kind and gentle. But Anna knew she was also dangerous. Mama and Daddy hated her and said if Anna wasn't careful, she could make it so Anna had to move away from them. It confused her, but she knew she only had to remind the nurse that she was clumsy and always falling down. The marks, she said, were from where Mama or Daddy tried to catch her and keep her from falling.

When she reached the office, Nurse Janey was hanging up the phone. She ushered Anna to a chair and popped a thermometer into her mouth. When it beeped, she said, "Normal," and smiled.

"Looks like you have some more ouchies," Nurse Janey said. "The back of your legs, and here on your arms again." She gently turned Anna's small body this way and that, looking at old bruises that were fading and new ones that were just blooming.

"What happened?" she asked again.

"Oh, that. I bumped into a chair," Anna explained, proud of herself for her quick response. She was good at thinking on her feet, and it helped that she was able to plan it with Ruthie.

The nurse nodded her head thoughtfully. She asked Anna to wait a moment while she wrote some things down. Anna worried about what she was writing, and Ruthie told her to scoot up and look. She managed to peek over her shoulder, but the nurse wrote cursive and neither Anna nor Ruthie could read cursive. Instead, she smiled her most calm and reasonable smile that said she knew she was just a silly little girl who was super clumsy.

The nurse looked at Anna, her eyes watering. Anna thought she looked like she was about to sneeze.

"Okay, sweetie," she said. "Back to class with you. Thank

you for talking to me. Do you want an ice pack for your bruises?"

"No," Anna said. She wasn't a little baby who needed an ice pack for every little bump. "I do this so much that I'm used to it." She thought she sounded very grown up and matter of fact as she said this. She was a mature six-year-old. Everyone said so.

Nurse Janey thumbed through her paperwork till she found the note with Lori's number on it. After the incident yesterday and now with these new bruises today, she had to make another call.

Within an hour, Lori Jamieson from the Department of Child Services poked her head into Nurse Janey's office. While she signed in and got a visitor's pass, Janey told her a little of what was going on.

"But," she said, "you really need to talk to Ms. Canter. She has more information about yesterday."

Curious about what happened yesterday, Lori quickly made her way to Anna's kindergarten classroom. Her heels clicked surprisingly loud on the tile hallway and echoed back to her.

When she reached the classroom, she paused to catch her breath. She tucked her short hair behind her ears and ran her ring fingers under her eyes. Her eyeliner always ran when she sweat. When she was ready, she moved to the classroom's window and waved until she caught the teacher's eye. Ms. Canter saw her and stood quickly, holding one finger up for her to wait a moment.

She whispered something to the classroom helper and then walked quickly to the door.

"Hey," she said, quietly closing the door behind her.

"Hi," Lori replied. "What's going on? Nurse Janey said to

talk to you first. Something happened yesterday?"

"Yes, it was strange. I asked Anna to bring me her homework paper. She hadn't done it which isn't too surprising. That happens a lot, and I know her situation, so I generally don't make a big deal of it. I planned to work on it with her."

Lori nodded her head and said, "Thanks for that."

"Of course. Anyway, I asked for her homework, and she started crying. Not just crying but sobbing and, well, kind of wailing. Like she was hurt or something. It was really loud and kind of scary. The other kids were freaked out," she added.

"What did she say afterward? Did she explain the breakdown?"

"No. In fact, we took her to the nurse, and she continued to wail and carry on for a few more minutes, then she got really quiet. And this is the strange part. She asked the nurse why she was there."

"She asked her why she was in the nurse's office?" Lori reiterated.

"Yes, it was like she didn't remember crying or being upset or even walking to the office. Almost like she was in a trance or something," Ms. Canter added.

"I'm guessing Nurse Janey didn't have any ideas either?" Lori asked.

"Nope. Something was obviously bothering her. Maybe she was just embarrassed by her reaction and didn't want to talk about it," Ms. Canter suggested.

Lori, hoping the answer was no but still having to ask, said, "Did you guys call the parents?"

Ms. Canter laughed and leaned in closer to Lori.

"That would only make things worse. We know better."

Lori smiled knowingly and Ms. Canter continued.

"We decided to wait since she did calm down, but then today, the new bruises. That's why we called you."

Lori nodded and thanked the teacher for her discretion

and common sense. "You guys are so wonderful here. I really appreciate all you do for Anna."

"I just hope you can get her into a safe place," the teacher said.

Lori thanked her for the information and asked if she could visit with Anna for a little while. It wasn't a normal visitation day, but as long as she was there, she wanted to see the little girl.

Ms. Canter went into the room and tapped Anna on the shoulder. She jumped and looked around quickly, eyes wide and scared. Ms. Canter pointed to Lori, who smiled and waved. When Anna saw Lori, her face broke into a wide grin. She put her book away and stowed her pencil in its tray, then ran for Lori.

"You're here," she said, throwing her arms around Lori's waist in a tight hug. Lori reached one arm down and hugged her back while making a point to get a good look at the black and blue bruises beginning to form on the back of her arms.

"I know! I was in the area and thought, 'gee, I wonder what Anna is up to?' so I decided to stop in. How are you doing?" she asked as they started their usual walk down the hallway.

"I'm really sleepy. I love school. I'm okay," she said.

This was the usual response. Lori had a hard time getting Anna to say things that bothered her and to process her feelings. Anna was much more likely to brush things off and say everything was okay than she was to face issues head on. This was a recipe for trouble later in life. Lori knew from her experience and her education that this stuff had to be dealt with.

"So, what happened yesterday?"

"What do you mean?" Anna asked.

"Well, they told me you were really upset. You were crying and went to the nurse. Remember?" Lori said.

"I went to the nurse today."

"I know. I'm thinking about yesterday though. Do you remember? You were crying and upset?"

"No. I'm okay," Anna said.

Lori wasn't convinced. She could tell something was off about the child. How did she not remember bursting into tears in the middle of her classroom? And if she did remember, why was she pretending it didn't happen?

She decided not to press the issue right now. Instead, she would make a home visit and hopefully Anna's parents could answer some of these questions for her.

After a short walk down the hall and back, she deposited Anna at her classroom door. Anna hugged her extra hard.

"Come visit me again, okay?" she said.

Lori promised she would visit again soon and waved one more time.

Before leaving the building, she stopped to sign out. She passed Nurse Janey in the office.

"I'll be seeing you," she said with a wave.

"Did you find out anything?" Nurse Janey asked.

"No, Anna told me the same thing she told you. Either she doesn't remember crying, or she is denying it happened for some reason. I didn't push her on it, but I'll be documenting it. For now, I'm heading to the house to see about those bruises."

"Sounds great. Thanks Lori," she said.

Lori hurried to her car. The parking lot was even hotter than normal for this fall day. She started her car and turned the air up high while she thought.

She needed to go back to the Marshall house as soon as possible. She generally gave the parents of her clients the benefit of the doubt, but she was finding it difficult to do that with this family. Obviously, something had triggered Anna's outburst, and she wanted to know what it was. This was new and it was scary. She didn't like it one bit, and she hoped she was wrong about the parents, and they would be willing to shed some light on the situation.

While she herself had never had a bad experience with a parent, some of her colleagues had been chased away with a gun or had their safety threatened in other ways.

She decided to visit after Anna got home that afternoon. That lessened the likelihood of an altercation happening. And she wanted to see Anna interact with her parents and see her in her home environment. She would also let the office know where she was, just in case.

Chapter 8
1983

Anna got off the school bus at the end of the dirt road. She turned and waved to the bus driver who waved back. She walked, kicking rocks and sticks as she came across them. Just before she followed the curve that took her out of sight of the main road, she heard the bus pull away. She knew the driver watched her until he couldn't see her any longer. One time he asked her how long the walk was and if she was scared of being alone. Anna didn't mind, and she told him so. She enjoyed the quiet walk. Plus, she wasn't really alone, but she didn't tell him that.

Despite the humidity and mugginess of the day, the air smelled fresh and clean. A cool breeze teased her and reminded Anna of the proper snow they had last year. She remembered measuring it with her ruler just outside the back door. She hoped for a foot, but it was only eight inches. Still it was exciting and the biggest snowfall she had seen. She even went out to play in it but not for too long. She didn't have snow boots or even a heavy coat. Her mittens were cheap yarn ones that barely kept her hands warm, much less dry.

She became aware of the sound of gravel crunching beneath her feet and knew she was getting closer to the house.

The gravel was probably an improvement when it was first put down. Before that the drive was a long stretch of dirt and when it rained, mud puddles. Ruthie told her that.

Anna liked to imagine her ancestors driving down this very path in a horse and carriage or a wagon even. Ruthie told her that she used to walk this path too, kicking rocks and stirring up dust just like Anna did now.

Anna knew Ruthie was an imaginary friend, and she figured her stories were imaginary too. But Ruthie didn't just tell Anna about things, she showed them to her. Anna would lose herself in Ruthie's stories and forget it was make-believe.

One of her favorites was when Ruthie found out her parents were going to the World's Columbian Exhibition. Anna asked Ms. Canter about it, and she told her it was a world's fair in Chicago in 1893. Anna couldn't believe Ruthie was so old.

Still, she loved seeing how excited Ruthie was when her Pa pulled up in his wagon. Ruthie imitated his deep voice and southern accent as she recited from memory, "Your reservations on the East Tennessee, Virginia, and Georgia Railroad are confirmed. Boarding on 26 June, 1893, arriving Chicago, Illinois. A room has been secured for you at The Ingram on Sixtieth Street. Returning 17 July, 1893, by the same route."

Ruthie told Anna about the wonderful things her parents would see at the fair. She talked about things like chewing gum and Coca-Cola and the electricity display. Anna didn't have the heart to tell her those things were no big deal. She already felt bad that Ruthie didn't get to go and had to stay home with her brother.

It was a good story, but Anna always felt sorry for Ruthie in the end. She wanted her to tell a happy story, but Ruthie didn't have many of those. Neither did Anna, so she understood.

Anna approached her house slowly. She listened for sounds of fighting from inside. It was quiet. She crept up the front steps, careful to avoid the places where rot had taken over. She barely registered the red spray-painted sign on the house warning visitors away. Mama made Daddy do it when they first got married because so many people heard about their ghosts and wanted to talk to them. It was too bad that their family had such good stories when they were the least likely people in the world to want to tell them to anyone.

She pulled the screen door open inch by inch, but it still squealed on its hinges. She opened it only enough to squeeze her small body through and then bolted up the stairs. She was hungry after school but knew enough to wait before she went to the kitchen. She got in trouble last week when she asked for a snack right after school. She didn't think she said that was all Mama was good for. She knew Mama did other things for her. Or at least she knew she was supposed to pretend that she did. And she didn't need or even want Mama to actually fix her something. She was going to do it herself.

Anna darted to her room and listened carefully to the sounds of the house. Creaks and groans were common. The house was old, and Daddy never fixed anything. Sometimes there was a loud crash when something fell over. She was usually blamed for that, so she definitely stayed put when that happened. Today she could hear talking. Mama and Daddy seemed to be in the living room, probably sitting on the couch since it was one of two pieces of furniture in the room. The other was a little table in front of the couch that held bottles and cigarettes and other things. They didn't sound angry, and Anna waited for the rise and fall of voices that signaled a pending argument. After several minutes of careful listening, she decided it was safe to go downstairs.

Just before she left her room, she stopped and listened again. She thought she heard a car. Anna looked out her upstairs window. A little red car moved slowly toward the house. Mama and Daddy hadn't heard it yet, and Anna wondered what would happen to the poor soul who dared approach their door. Most likely he or she would see the sign and leave. That's what usually happened.

Anna decided to wait it out a little longer. If Mama and Daddy realized someone was trespassing, it would make them angry, even if the person didn't get out of their car. If they got angry at someone for anything, they usually yelled at her, so she made sure to stay far out of the way.

She moved from the window and tiptoed to her closet. Her doll sat patiently, propped up just outside the closet door where Anna could see her. Her name was Ruthie. Just like her imaginary friend.

Anna crawled into her closet and settled onto a small nest of pillows and a blanket. She leaned against the wall and found a book to read. Even in the back of the closet, she still had enough daylight to read easily.

When they heard the loud knock at the door, Amber and David looked at each other. Who could be knocking and why didn't they hear them drive up? David sighed as he climbed out of the sunken couch cushion and shuffled to the door. It opened with a familiar creak and then Amber heard him talking. She listened carefully but couldn't tell who it was.

They didn't have any friends and they had spray painted "keep out" on the front door. The few idiots who dared knock despite the sign soon learned they meant what they said. She couldn't imagine who had the nerve to interrupt their evening by banging on their door. Finally, curiosity got the better of her. She heaved herself off of the couch.

"Oh, what the hell?" she mumbled as she made her way down the hallway. David stood with his arm across the doorway, talking to a woman. His arm made it difficult for Amber to see who the woman was, so she stood just behind him and tried to peer over his shoulder.

"Like I said, Mr. Marshall. I'd just like to ask you a few questions and then talk to Anna for a few minutes, alone."

"Well, I don't think that's going to happen, missy. Who sent you here and why?" David demanded.

Amber stood on her tiptoes and stretched her neck still trying to see over and around David. She thought it was the same woman who came earlier this year and made them send Anna to school. Lori something.

"Again, Mr. Marshall, I can't tell you who sent me, but someone close to Anna has expressed concern about the marks and bruises on her body. We just want to make sure she is safe," she said.

"I know you," Amber butted in loudly. It was the same woman. She was sure of it. "You got a search warrant this time?" she asked.

David looked over his shoulder with narrowed eyes. She knew that look meant shut up and do it now. Amber slunk back and put one hand over her mouth and made a tight fist with the other one at her side. She briefly locked eyes with the woman at the door and then looked away.

"Sir, I will come back with an officer if I need to, but wouldn't it be easier to just let me talk to Anna for a few minutes? Let me see her so I can mark that she is okay, and I've done my job. She is okay, isn't she?" Lori asked.

The way she blinked her wide eyes and smiled made Amber want to hit her. But it worked and David moved his arm. He nudged Amber out of the way.

"Be my guest," he said, sweeping his arm along the hallway, he bowed his head and let Lori in. He was being a smart ass. Amber knew it and wondered if the woman, Lori, knew it too.

Amber watched her look around. She could tell Lori was judging her just because they didn't have money to fix the torn water-stained wallpaper or replace the threadbare rug in the hallway. When she looked at her house through that woman's eyes, she became angry and defensive. Her house was no doubt bigger than the woman's, and they had land too. That was worth something. Amber justified her thoughts and fixed a glare on the uppity woman who came to judge her.

Despite the obvious age of the house and the wear and tear that nature and neglect had imposed, Lori knew the house used to be beautiful. She could see the history in the old wood and brick. And there was another feeling. A strange sort of vibe of old souls lurking around. Her thoughts were interrupted when she noticed the dirty dishes all over the place along with empty pizza boxes, and it looked like David chewed tobacco and had a terrible aim when it came time to spit. She tried not to vomit and forced a smile.

"Can I see Anna's room?" she asked.

Amber grumbled, "This way, busy body bitch."

Lori heard what she said but stayed quiet and followed Amber halfway up the stairs where she stopped abruptly. Lori managed to avoid bumping into her on the narrow staircase. She jumped when Amber shouted.

"Anna!"

Amber leaned forward and yelled again.

"Anna! A woman is coming up," she looked at Lori. "Go on then. Get it over with and leave."

As Amber started back down the stairs, Lori tried to move out of the way. There wasn't much room for the two of them to pass each other, but Amber was determined to go back down. Lori pressed herself to the wall and sucked in her breath as Amber thudded past her. When she reached the bottom stair, she sat with a grunt.

Good, Lori thought, *you stay right there.*

She realized she'd been holding her breath and let out a sigh as she climbed the rest of the stairs. When she reached the top, she could see Anna peeking through a slightly opened door.

Lori put her finger to her lips and whispered, "Let's talk in your room."

Anna nodded wisely and opened the door wider so Lori could come in. She picked up her doll and crawled onto her bed while Lori struggled to close the door.

It was a heavy door, and it hung loosely in its hinges. Lori noted there was a lock on the outside of the door, but not on the inside. Not a good sign. She hated parents like this. They figured they could bully and abuse their children so they could bully and abuse anyone else they disliked.

Anna put her finger to her lips.

"Hi," Lori whispered. "Do we need to be quiet even with the door closed?"

Anna nodded and pointed down.

"Sometimes they can hear me even when I try to be quiet."

Lori nodded. Sounds traveled easily in old houses like this one, and she wouldn't have been surprised at all to find David and Amber directly below them, listening through the ceiling.

"Why are you here?" Anna asked. "I didn't know you were coming to see me after school."

"I wanted to see your room," Lori said. "Who's this?" she asked, pointing to Anna's doll. She shuddered slightly at the sight of the doll. It was very old and creepy. Lori felt bad, but there was just no other word for it.

"Ruthie," Anna said proudly.

"That's a pretty name," Lori said. "How did you pick it?"

"I named her after my imaginary friend."

"Did your parents give her to you?" Lori asked.

"I found her. In a box. In the attic."

"Do you spend a lot of time in the attic?"

Anna looked away and shook her head slightly. She seemed to be struggling with an answer. Lori didn't want to put her on the spot, so she changed the subject.

"What do you like to do when you're at home? With your parents?" Lori questioned.

"Nothing. We mostly stay in here," Anna replied.

Lori started to ask her next question when she paused and looked thoughtful.

"Who do you mean when you say 'we'?" she wondered.

"Me and my toys and Ruthie," Anna said. Her voice trailed off as she looked around her empty room.

Lori did the same and felt a pang of sorrow for this little girl. The bruises didn't lie. But the room, although sparse and threadbare, was mostly clean. And even though the house was piled with stuff, she didn't see bugs or rodents or the leavings of either, at least not in this room. Anna looked fed, although small for sure. But that didn't mean she wasn't eating, she could just be really small. She was definitely a sad little girl, and Lori had no doubt her parents hurt her. She was lonely too. But, Lori reminded herself, at least she had her creepy, weird doll to keep her company.

"What do you usually eat for dinner?"

Anna thought for a few moments.

"Grilled cheese sandwiches with the cheese oozing out. And ice cream. And I love gumbo," she said.

"Gumbo! Does your Mama make that for you?" Lori asked.

Anna shook her head.

"I used to make grilled cheese for myself, but now the stove doesn't work good. Mama says it's 'fend for yourself night' most nights, so I usually make cold cheese sandwiches. Sometimes we have crackers," Anna stated.

"When do you get to eat your yummy gumbo?"

Anna's eyes lit up, and she smiled showing a missing front tooth. "At my Aunt Lu and Aunt Jody's house. I love visiting them! We always watch cartoons, and they have movies too. And I can eat as much as I want. And the bed I sleep in, I have my own room there too, it is really soft, and the sheets always smell so good. Like, um, what's that called? It's purple? They smell like purple."

Lori was taken aback at the sudden enthusiasm in Anna. She had never seen the child's eyes light up like they were now. She smiled at Anna's exuberance and then tried to think of what a six-year-old thinks 'purple' smells like. Then it hit her.

"Oh! You mean lavender," she guessed.

"Yes!" Anna confirmed.

"Okay, kiddo. Thank you for letting me visit," Lori stood and then smoothed the sheets where she had been sitting.

"Are you leaving so soon?" Anna asked.

"Yes, I'm afraid so," Lori said. "But I'll see you at school next week, and I might come by and visit here again. Would that be all right with you?"

Anna nodded. Lori knew her school visits meant a lot to Anna. It was one of the few times she was made to feel special.

"Do you want to walk down with me?"

Anna shook her head.

"Okay then. See you soon," she assured her with a quick hug.

Lori left the bedroom and picked her way down the stairs. She worried about leaving Anna upstairs alone. But her thoughts shifted quickly when she saw Amber and David waiting at the foot of the staircase.

"I have a few questions for you both," she said and started back towards the living area before they could say anything.

Amber followed close on her heels. Lori could tell she was getting angry, but she didn't care.

David was acting calmer than his wife, but Lori didn't like the way he looked at her either. Trying to diffuse the tension, she asked if they could sit for a moment and talk.

"No, I think we'll just stand here. I don't want you coming in here and getting too comfortable on my couch. And you won't be staying that long anyway," David informed her.

Lori nodded. She wasn't going to challenge this scary man and his weird wife. And really, she didn't want to sit on their furniture. She feared what she might sit in. She glanced at the table strewn with empty liquor bottles, mirrors and straws and noticed a needle peeking out from under the couch. Her stomach flipped.

Normally, she liked to get to know the parents she worked with. She viewed her job as a partner to families. Most of the time the parents just needed some guidance. Young, uneducated, and from challenging childhoods themselves, they were just doing what they knew to do. They genuinely loved their children and wanted what was best for them. They simply needed to be taught how to parent.

In this case though, her help was clearly not wanted. These two were arrogant and stubborn. She could tell they had no interest in learning how to become better parents. They acted like they were perfect, and her presence was an unwelcome interference. Lori got to the business at hand.

"As I said before, I'm here because someone who knows Anna was concerned with the bruises on her arms. It looks as though someone grabbed her pretty hard," Lori began but was quickly interrupted.

"You saying I'm beating my kid?" challenged David.

"Actually, no. I didn't say that at all. I said someone who knows Anna was concerned about the bruises on her arms," Lori tried to keep the exasperation out of her voice.

"I'm here to make sure she is okay and to make sure you know about the bruises. Most parents would want to make sure their child was okay and would be concerned," Lori finished. Her last words hung in the air, and she waited for one of them to at least ask if their child was okay.

They both just stood, looking at Lori.

Finally, David said, "She's always running into things, isn't she?" he looked at Amber.

"She's the clumsiest kid ever," Amber added. "Always

running into doors and walls and falling on the stairs and stuff."

They heard a noise, and all three turned toward the hallway. Anna stood there, her face red. She had dropped the book she was holding and bent down to pick it up.

David and Amber both yelled at the same time, "Go to your room!" and Anna scurried away quickly.

"Well, she seems to listen to you pretty well," Lori said with more than a touch of sarcasm.

"Okay, that's enough," David stated. In a few quick strides, he was at the front door. He opened it wide.

"Bye," he said.

Lori walked to the door slowly. She was ready to leave, but she wanted to have the upper hand and put these people on notice.

"I will be visiting again in a few weeks. And I'll be talking to Anna regularly. The bruises are serious, and we won't be ignoring them. I try to give parents the benefit of the doubt but..." her words trailed off as she looked pointedly at both of them.

Lori moved through the door and stood on the porch. Once a proud feature of the house, it now sagged in both corners and even had a few holes where obvious wood rot took someone's foot right through. She placed her feet where the planks looked healthier and continued.

"You might try reading with Anna or even just talking to her. She seems very lonely. I'd also like to see her visiting with her aunts a little more. She seems to really enjoy being with them," she said.

David screwed up his face and spat out, "Lesbians!"

Amber snorted and rolled her eyes.

"Well, their personal life is of no interest to me. They are obviously very kind to Anna, and that is what is important here," Lori said.

She had had enough of these ignorant people who

couldn't be bothered to do anything beneficial for their child. She also had that gnawing feeling in her gut that told her if she stayed much longer, she would end up antagonizing these parents and picking a fight. It was the worst part of her job when she ran into people like this.

Stupid, ignorant bullies, she thought as she slowly picked her way down the rotted steps. She stopped when she heard the shattering of glass and turned back stunned.

"Did you just throw something at me?" she asked incredulously.

Amber and David stood with their mouths open, looking at the floor of the porch. Five beer bottles had stood in a row on the railing. Now they were a pile of glass glittering in front of the Marshalls.

Lori quickly realized they hadn't thrown anything at her. Most likely they broke them out of frustration or anger. It was an immature response and didn't surprise her at all.

As she opened her car door, she called back over her shoulder, "I'll see you in a few weeks. Take care of your daughter."

"Not if I see you first," Amber said just loud enough for Lori to hear. David pushed her inside and slammed the door shut.

Lori got into her car and exhaled. She felt like she'd been holding her breath the entire time she was in that house. Such a gloomy and dank place. The feel of the whole house was depressing and sad and...evil. Her mind didn't usually go there, but the feeling was so overwhelming. She wished there was an alternative for Anna. Somewhere bright and cheery where she would be happy and cared for. Something was definitely off about that child. She couldn't quite put her finger on it.

She drove to the office to file her paperwork and to schedule her next visit to the Marshall house.

"Anna! Get down here," Daddy yelled.

Anna scampered down the stairs. She knew she would be called down and was ready. Either they wanted to know what she and Miss Lori talked about, or they were going to yell at her for coming down with the book. Or maybe both.

She went into the room where her parents were waiting. They sat side by side on the couch. Mama on the good side that didn't sink, had her arms folded over her chest. Daddy on his side, but instead of letting the couch swallow his body like usual, he was sitting forward with his forearms on his knees.

"What did you say to that woman?" he asked without preamble.

"Nothing," Anna said.

"Well, now we know it wasn't nothing. She was in there with you a long time. What did you say to her? What did she say to you?" he asked.

Anna thought hard. She needed to start talking soon because she'd learned that when she was quiet, they thought she was up to something. Sometimes she could tell a joke or say something funny, and it would help fill the silence and even make them laugh. But she knew that wasn't the thing to do right now.

She felt a nudge from Ruthie and shook her head, trying to clear her mind and form an answer they would accept.

"Are you telling me no?" Daddy asked.

"Answer the question," demanded Mama.

"We talked about what I like to do," Anna said quickly. "I told her I like to read. She asked me if I like Aunt Lu, and I said yes," Anna racked her brain for anything else to say, or not to say.

"Did she ask you about being clumsy?" Mama asked.

Daddy shot her a look, and she looked down at her hands.

"Um, no," Anna said. "We didn't talk about that. Just stuff I like. Oh! And what I like to eat for dinner too. We talked about that," Anna finished.

She thought her answers were pretty good. Her parents didn't look angry. She enjoyed visiting with Lori and looked forward to seeing her at school. She wasn't going to tell her parents that though. She knew that would be the one thing that would make them angry.

"Just so you know, if you tell her bad things about us, she will take you away from us," Daddy said. He smiled with his thin lips pushed together.

Anna's heart jumped. Her first thought was that she could live with Aunt Lu and Aunt Jody. She knew she would love that.

"And before you go getting all excited thinking you'd be living with your good for nothing aunt, don't even think it." It was like Mama read her mind.

"Naw, it wouldn't be someone you like, that's for sure," Daddy piled on. "It would be someone who wouldn't be nice to you at all. They wouldn't care about you. Probably stuff you in a room with a bunch of other kids. No new clothes. No food. You would hate it."

Anna nodded and tried to look thoughtful. She didn't want to live in a room with a bunch of other kids.

"Okay, Daddy," she said.

Anna paused waiting for her parents to say something else. Daddy lit a cigarette. Mama poured some of that clear stuff that looked like water, but definitely wasn't, into their glasses. Anna was pretty sure they had forgotten she was standing there, so she slowly turned and tiptoed back to her room. Once there, she closed the door and sighed. Remembering how Miss Lori struggled with the door, Anna made a mental note to show her how to work it. There was a trick to it.

She crawled onto her bed and gathered Ruthie into her arms. With her eyes closed, she made herself relax and think good thoughts. She felt like she just barely escaped being in big trouble and was getting tired. It was always that way. She was always tired. She did kind of want to leave her house, but only to go to Aunt Lu's. And she was pretty sure there was no way to make that happen.

As she daydreamed about living with Aunt Lu and Aunt Jody, Ruthie interrupted her thoughts.

You could, swirled through her mind.

Anna played along with her imagination and asked, "How?"

Only one word appeared to her. She felt it as much as she saw it.

Fire.

Chapter 9
1983

That night, Lu got a call from her friend, Monique. Monique was the school secretary at Anna's elementary school. She wanted to let Lu know that Lori Jamieson came to the school again and said she was going to the house that afternoon.

"I don't know what ended up happening," she said. "But I knew you would want to know."

Lu thanked her old friend for the call and carefully copied down the name of the Department of Child Services representative who was brave enough to visit the Marshall's house.

She checked her watch. It was almost six o'clock. Unlikely anyone would answer but Lu decided to call anyway and leave a message.

Lori answered after the second ring. After a brief hesitation, Lu told her who she was.

"I hope you will talk to me about Anna," she said after introductions. "Technically I'm not her guardian, but I am one of the few people who care about her."

The line was quiet for a few seconds and then Lori began to speak.

"I just came from the house," she said softly. "I will talk to you."

As Lori told Lu about her visit, Lu became more and more worried about Anna's safety and even worried about Lori's safety, too.

"They aren't stable," Lu said cautiously.

"Oh, I definitely got that impression," Lori said.

"I suppose the school called you because of the bruises?" she asked.

"Yes, that and what happened yesterday. Did you hear about that? She started crying and went to the nurse. When we asked her about it, she acted like she had no idea what we were talking about," Lori said.

"No, I hadn't heard, but that doesn't surprise me. There's lots of things she doesn't seem to remember, and she doesn't tell us anything either. She drives me crazy when she goes into her routine saying she's clumsy and bumps into things. But you've seen the bruises, right? They are from a hand - fingers," Lu said.

"Yes, I saw them. She tells me the same thing. It looks like she tells everyone the same thing. I'll keep trying. It might take a little longer, but eventually, she'll start talking to one of us," Lori said.

"Has she told you about her imaginary friend? When she visits, we can hear her talking in her room. We've listened a few times. I think she's actually talking to the doll. It's a full conversation, like she hears the doll talking and then she answers it. Should we be concerned?"

"No, I don't think so. I got to meet Ruthie today, actually. I think Anna finds comfort in her. The conversations she has are probably her way of processing what's going on, in her head and in real life. We know she is lonely and Ruthie, the doll and the imaginary friend, keep her company and probably help her make sense of her surroundings. Honestly, I think that's the least of our worries," Lori reassured her.

"Okay. I'm going to go ahead and say this too, my partner and I have talked about it and if there is any chance Anna could live with us, we would take her in a heartbeat. Is there any way that could happen?" Lu held her breath waiting for the answer.

There was another long pause, and then Lori spoke slowly, measuring her words carefully.

"It's tricky. Technically, Anna is being cared for. She's fed and clothed. They get her to school regularly now. The house is..." Lori paused and then continued. "I have to make a good case to remove a child. And while you and I both know she's being abused, it's a tough thing to remove a child from the parents. We have a lot of suspicions but not much proof. Especially since Anna won't say anything."

"Even with the drug use?" Lu asked.

"They make no effort to hide it, do they?" Lori said. "Drug paraphernalia was everywhere when I was there. I have reported it to the local police, and they are watching, but again, I'm not the police. I can't arrest them, and the police can't just show up there and search the house. So, we are left in limbo. For right now anyway," she added quickly.

"I understand," Lu said.

"One more thing. When I left, I could hear them shouting at Anna before I even got to my car. I think it would be very good for her to spend as much time as possible with you. I feel like she was in trouble just because I visited," she added.

"I understand. We love having her here," Lu agreed.

"Maybe this weekend, if you can," she suggested.

"Absolutely," Lu said. Then she sighed heavily. There was something she wanted Lori Jamieson to know. Something she hadn't told anyone before, but if it would help Anna, she would talk about it.

"I have one more thing to tell you about David. Maybe it will help you make your case."

The next day, while Anna was at school, Lu called the house.

David answered with a groggy, "Yeah."

"I'm getting Anna this weekend," she stated. "I'll pick her up from school today."

"Yeah, yeah," David mumbled again. He was drunk or high in the middle of the day, most likely both and probably wouldn't remember this conversation at all. She wondered if he would miss Anna over the weekend. If he would even realize she wasn't there. If so, would he wonder where she was? Probably not.

Lu hung up the phone in disgust. No time for that. She had to get ready for Anna's visit. Abhay was visiting too, and she and Jody wanted it to be perfect. She ran through a checklist in her mind. Anna had enough clothes at the house for the weekend. They just grocery shopped for Abhay's visit, so there was plenty of food for little kids. They had chicken nuggets, mac n cheese, and everything to make grilled cheese, with the cheese oozing out, of course. The room they stayed in had bunk beds that were always made up and ready for them. All she had to do was pick Anna up as soon as school let out. She needed to make sure the school knew not to let Anna get on the bus.

"Wonderful!" Jody squealed when Lu told her Anna would be staying with them too. "Now the kids can finally spend some time getting to know each other! The timing is perfect!"

Lu smiled. Jody loved to play house. With no children of their own, they spent as much time as possible with their niece and nephew. And it was even better now that Abhay's family moved to Tennessee. They were able to see him even more often which thrilled Jody. It also gave her the opportunity to revive her relationship with her oldest sister, May.

Lu still felt responsible for the falling out between Jody

and Lynda, so she was particularly invested in helping Jody and May smooth things over. Lu hoped May could see Jody's love for her son, and it would help erase the hurt and bitterness between them. Abhay and Anna were the link that could potentially bring the three sisters back together. Making Jody happy and easing Lu's guilt.

As the end of the school day approached, Lu waited patiently in the office. She talked to Monique in between phone calls and busy students with questions. Anna's teacher knew to tell Anna not to get on the bus and to go straight to the office instead.

Lu still worried about missing her, so she was there before the last bell rang. She stood at the door and scanned the kids as they streamed past her, watching for Anna.

Most of the kids wore shorts and t-shirts and some of the girls wore simple cotton dresses. Almost all the little girls had their hair pulled up into lopsided ponytails tied with ribbons on the verge of falling out. Most every boy had shoelaces dangling dangerously on the ground as they walked quickly, just shy of a run. Their brightly colored backpacks, advertising a wide assortment of cartoon characters and superheroes, were bursting with notebooks and papers, lunch boxes, and unused jackets.

Lu smiled as she watched them. Little kids were so cute. But when she finally saw Anna, her heart skipped a beat. Anna walked slowly. The other kids rushed past her, but she seemed to not notice them. She was smaller than most of the other kindergarteners, easily ten pounds less than the average. Her backpack was adult size, black and dirty, and bumped into the back of her knees as she walked. Her hair was tangled and hung straight down, no bows, and her clothes looked shabby. She wore a long-sleeved shirt despite the heat. Lu briefly wondered what new bruises lived under those sleeves. She decided the first thing she would do is give the girl a bath and burn those clothes.

And put a bow in her hair, just because, Lu thought.

Lu watched Anna's face register panic as she tried to cross the stream of students to go into the office. When she was close to earshot, Lu called her name. Anna searched the crowd and when her eyes met Lu's, her face lit up. She burst into a run, dodging through the other students, and flung herself into Lu's arms.

"I didn't know you were getting me today!" she said.

"Yup! You're spending the whole weekend with us," Lu said happily.

They held hands as they walked to Lu's little, white Mazda. Anna climbed into the back and buckled herself into her booster seat.

"Let's go," she said, and Lu smiled at her in the rearview mirror.

"So, how's it going kiddo?" she asked, pulling out of the school's drive. She ignored the jerk tailgating her in the 15 mph school zone and deliberately went a tiny bit slower.

"Nothing much, Aunt Lu," Anna said. "Is Jody at home?"

"Yep! You got both of us all weekend. We're going to eat and shop and snuggle and watch movies and read books! And, guess what? Abhay is there too!" Lu announced.

"Yay!" Anna said and clapped her hands.

Lu smiled remembering how hard Anna practiced saying his name and how patient Jody was with teaching her.

"Uh-bye," Jody had said, breaking it down for her when Anna was only three. They stood in front of one of his pictures. Anna was fascinated by his dark complexion and huge brown eyes. Mostly it was his smile though. It lit up his face and Anna responded to his picture with an equally big smile every time she passed.

Lu pulled into the driveway of their quaint cottage. It was tucked into the back of a small subdivision on the edge of town. Their house didn't look like the other houses around them and that suited them just fine. It was smaller by half than the average house, and they had a large yard they had let go natural. Jody joked that "letting it go natural" isn't exactly what happened.

"It takes a lot of work to make your yard look like it doesn't take any work," she always said whenever someone commented on the beautiful native flowers and plants that tangled themselves across the ground.

When they walked into the house, Anna screamed with joy.

"I smell gumbo!"

"Anything for you kid," Jody said as she gave Anna a hug.

As she hugged Aunt Jody, Anna looked over her shoulder at Abhay. He stood awkwardly, watching her and Jody. Then he smiled. Anna immediately smiled back. She reached for Abhay, and the young children embraced as though they had known each other their whole lives.

Chapter 10
2019

"Hello Anna," Carla cooed as soon as Anna walked into the school building.

"Hey," she replied as she quickly moved past her colleague.

She gritted her teeth and tried not to outwardly cringe. As a general rule, Anna didn't hate people, but this woman challenged that daily. She second guessed everything Anna did for her special needs students. She had no idea what Anna's job entailed and had no desire to learn. Most of the students didn't like her because she demanded much more from them than they were remotely capable of giving. And she mocked them. Anna couldn't stand that, and it put her on edge immediately.

She managed to avoid being pulled into a conversation and got away as quickly as possible. Still, as she started down the long hallway to her classroom, she felt the physical manifestation of her suppressed emotions. As she walked, the hallway started to shift, and her vision grew hazy. She slowed down as the floor tilted at an alarming angle. Her first thought was that they were having an earthquake, but she quickly realized it wasn't the floor tilting, it was her. She put a hand on the wall and steadied herself, taking deep breaths. Walking slowly and staying close to the wall for support, Anna stumbled through the building.

When she finally reached her classroom door, she leaned on the wall and rubbed her eyes. She rummaged through her bag looking for her keys. When she found the key ring, she paused, key in hand, and stared at the lock.

Which way does the key go? she thought. *Teeth up or down?*

She tried it both ways and still couldn't get the key in. She shook her head impatiently and tried to clear her mind to focus. She tried again, both ways, and sighed.

Okay, she thought. *Maybe the lock is broken.*

Forcing herself to relax and try one more time, she suddenly smiled to herself. This was her house key, not the school key. She fished around in her bag again and this time came up with the correct key attached to her ID lanyard. She noted that this would be a funny story to tell later, but her smile faded quickly when she was again faced with the question of how to put the key in the lock.

After a few tries, she managed to get the key in. A short debate with herself on which way to turn it ended with success. She marveled that the simplest thing she did every day for years took what seemed like an hour.

Anna made her way into her classroom, left the light off and sat at her desk. Her skin was crawling. She shuddered and rubbed the goosebumps on her arms. It felt like tiny bugs were swarming over her arms and head. She vaguely wondered if she was getting sick. It was flu season.

Next thing she realized, she was calling the office to say she was leaving. It wasn't a conscious decision to leave. She didn't remember thinking it through or coming to the decision herself. It happened first and then she became aware. She knew in a flash what was going on. Ruthie!

As always though, when Ruthie commanded something, Anna obeyed. She left a message for the office when no one answered the phone. She sent a few emails to critical people so they would know not to expect her that day. Then she left.

She was suddenly aware that she was driving her car.

How did I get here? she thought. *Did I talk to anyone?*

Her mind wasn't her own. She tried to take back control and decide where to go. Hospital emergency room? Walk in clinic? Home? Picking one was impossible. She panicked when she didn't recognize the route she was on. This was the same route she took both ways every single day for years. Now nothing looked familiar. She was lost.

Her eyes snapped open. Somehow, she had gotten from the car to this room. She quickly took inventory of her surroundings, trying to figure out where she was and what had happened. She was lying on a bed, under a warm blanket, with wires attached to her chest. A nurse was busy at a counter with her back to Anna. She was talking to her as though they had been having a conversation.

When the nurse turned back to her, Anna smiled. She was compliant as the nurse drew blood. Anna thought she seemed inappropriately chipper when she said she was checking for damage to the heart.

"We don't play around with chest pain," she explained. "How are you feeling now?"

"Fuzzy," Anna said. She closed her eyes and tried to remember to breathe.

"Do you want us to call anyone for you," she asked. "You'll need to stay here for a while until your vitals return to normal and we get some test results back."

"No, thanks," she stated. "I just want to rest."

"I'll be back shortly," the nurse said. She turned off the light and pulled the door but left it partly open.

Anna took a quick inventory. She was safe. No one else seemed to be hurt. She was with professionals. Anna fought to keep her eyes open, but she quickly succumbed to sleep. She slept soundly until she became aware of someone holding her hand. She opened one eye to see Abhay standing beside her. He was talking to someone in the room.

"Looks like a panic attack," she heard a voice saying. "But I want her to follow up with her doctor. This was a pretty bad one."

"Will do," Abhay said. "Oh, there you are." He smiled at her. "How are you feeling?"

The doctor came to her side, and the two men helped her sit up. Abhay kept a protective arm around her while the doctor checked her blood pressure and heart rate.

"How did you know?" Anna asked Abhay.

"It's really strange. I got a weird feeling that something was wrong. It was a very strong sensation that I couldn't ignore. I tried not to be paranoid or panic, but when I called to check on you, you didn't answer or call me back. So, I got worried and started looking for you," he said.

"But how did you know I was here?"

"Remember the location app we got on our phones?"

"Stalker," Anna said and smiled.

Abhay laughed.

"Should we cancel The Aunts?" he asked.

"No," Anna said quickly. "I've been looking forward to seeing them. And Lily would be furious."

"You're right," Abhay agreed. "They will definitely want to see you, probably even more so now. As long as you feel up to it. I'll call and let them know what happened though."

"You can go now," the doctor said. "I am very serious about following up with your doctor. You shouldn't have driven in that state. You're lucky. Go home, rest. You should feel better soon."

Abhay shook hands with the doctor and helped Anna from the table.

"We'll leave your car here and get it tomorrow," he said on their way to the check-out desk.

"No, that's crazy. I can drive," Anna protested weakly. "And I'll need it for work tomorrow."

"Yeah, right," he said. "You're not going to work tomorrow. I'm not having you end up in the hospital."

"Okay, you're right. I'll take it easy. No way I'm going to another hospital. I hate hospitals," she said.

"I know," Abhay said. "I remember."

Chapter 11
2019

Lu hung up the phone. She sighed heavily as she chose a bottle of sauvignon blanc and two glasses. She went in search of Jody and found her on the patio. It was a hot day, and she was sweating profusely. Her long, grey hair was in a bun and her long legs were stretched out, crossed at the ankles. Lu envied her height and slight build. Even when hot and sweaty, she managed to appear elegant. She hated to interrupt Jody's relaxation and hoped the wine would be welcomed.

Jody opened her eyes when she heard Lu come through the door.

"Nice," she said when she saw the wine. "Thanks. This is perfect."

"Not for long," Lu said. She poured two glasses and handed one to Jody.

"What's wrong?" Jody asked.

She sat up and leaned towards Lu, but Lu avoided eye contact. She looked at the backyard and sighed again.

"I just can't seem to get away from him," she said.

"It's hard to get away from family," Jody said. "Even when they're dead."

Lu was grateful that Jody knew exactly who she was talking about. She was more empathic than she realized.

"He's not my family. He's a curse on my life and always has been. Now he's a curse on Anna's life too. You are my family," she reached over and took Jody's hand.

"Has something come up?" Jody asked carefully.

"No, not really. I'm just thinking," Lu replied.

Jody opened her mouth to ask another question, but before she could, Lu changed the subject.

"Abhay called," she said.

"Making plans for our visit?" Jody asked.

"Not exactly. He was letting us know Anna was in the hospital for an anxiety attack. And he also wanted us to know that she's admitted to hearing Ruthie," Lu said. Her voice was flat and tired.

She had long suspected Anna still heard Ruthie even though she denied it. Ever since that day in therapy shortly after the fire, Lu realized that even though Anna stopped talking about Ruthie, that didn't mean she wasn't still hearing her. Lu blamed herself. Anna obviously picked up on how much it upset Lu when she talked to Ruthie. Lu never believed Ruthie was only an imaginary friend, and Anna sensed that. It wasn't that simple or innocent. She just didn't want to admit it.

"Oh, no," Jody said.

"I need to tell you something important," Lu said quietly.

"Okay," Jody sat back in her chair and waited for Lu to continue.

"Remember when we had Anna seeing a therapist just after the fire?" she asked.

Jody nodded.

"I never told you, but she overheard the doctor and me talking about the fire. The doctor made the suggestion that Anna started it. That her trauma was so great that she somehow started the fire, killed her parents and then blocked it all out," Lu said. Tears were threatening to spill, and she talked faster.

"Oh!" Jody said. She sat forward and looked intently at Lu.

"The doctor wanted to keep seeing her. She wanted to make Anna face all the things we suspected happened to her. But..." Lu choked on a sob.

"It was bringing up things for you too, wasn't it?" Jody asked. She took Lu's hand and cried with her.

When she could talk through the sobs, Lu blew her nose and continued.

"I'm afraid it's all my fault. If I had allowed that doctor to continue, Anna would have dealt with all of this years ago and not be having problems now. I've allowed her to go through life thinking she killed her parents in a fire that she set. All because I didn't want to remember or face my own issues. What kind of monster am I?" Lu cried out. She covered her face with her hands and began to cry again.

"Do you believe that?" Jody asked. "I mean, do you really think Anna did that? Really?"

Lu shook her head.

"No, I don't. I didn't then and I don't now. But it doesn't matter what we think, does it? It's what Anna thinks. She knows something happened to her but doesn't remember what it was, and she thinks she started that fire. What kind of life is that? I made her go through life like that," Lu said.

The women sat in silence for several minutes, each lost in her own thoughts, sipping her wine and occasionally blowing her nose.

"I think Anna has had a good life," Jody began, speaking slowly and choosing her words carefully. "I think what happened to her as a child certainly had an effect on her as an adult, but that's true for anyone. And, I think..." Jody hesitated.

Lu looked at her.

"Go on," she said.

"There's more to Ruthie than we know," Jody said. "And I know you know that. It's not so much about how the fire started. It's more about who or what Ruthie is. I mean, come on Lu, she hears a voice? In her head? And apparently has for her whole life? You know as well as anyone that strange things happened in that house all the time. Maybe Ruthie is another one of those strange things."

Lu nodded. She knew exactly what Jody was trying to say. Jody always thought the house was haunted, and Ruthie was a ghost. She would have pursued it if Lu had let her. Maybe it was time to let her.

"Call Lynda," Lu said.

"Really?" Jody asked. "Call her about Ruthie or call her just to talk?"

Lu laughed. She knew Jody was trying to lighten the mood, but she also wanted to be certain. This had been a sore spot between them for decades.

"Call her about Ruthie. See what she thinks. In the meantime, I'll talk to Anna. Tell her what I know. It's time to get all this out in the open," Lu concluded.

"I'll do it!" Jody said. She put her feet up and leaned back in her chair again. Then she asked, "So is Anna okay, after the anxiety attack?"

"Abhay said she's doing well. He said her psychiatrist thinks she's having some kind of PTSD triggered from seeing a few kids at the school who remind her of herself. And a CPS person came by which, of course, reminded her of Lori. So those things coupled with her lack of memory seems to have fed into it all. The medical doctor said she was okay. Not a heart attack or anything, but a pretty significant anxiety attack," Lu summed up their conversation.

"Do you think she remembered anything about Lori?" Jody asked.

"No. I'm not sure she even knows anything to remember.

I think it's buried with all the other stuff. I guess if she ever went looking for information, she could find some sort of record of it all. But I don't know if she would even think to look it up. All she knows is Lori went missing, maybe moved away. And I'm not sure the police ever officially charged Amber and David. Can you charge a dead person?" Lu asked rhetorically.

They sat in silence, Lu's question hanging in the air between them.

"Tell her," Jody finally said.

Lu nodded. She sank into silence as she thought about how she would tell Anna the horrors that happened in her home in the first six years of her life.

"She deserves to know everything," Lu agreed.

"Everything?" Jody asked.

"Everything," Lu said glumly.

Jody trusted that Lu meant what she said, but she wasn't sure she viewed 'everything' the same way Jody did.

The last time they talked about telling Anna everything, Lu was adamant that there was a limit to what she would share with Anna.

Lu had gone back into the house to call Abhay. She was going to finalize plans for them to visit the kids that coming weekend. Jody stayed outside and sipped her wine. She thought about what Lu confessed just a few minutes ago. Her mind returned to that day in the hospital, just before the fire.

She and Lu had just returned home from the hospital, still fuming over the act Amber put on.

"You know he's still there. You know he's going to do it again, right?" Lu kept asking her.

Jody just nodded her head and allowed Lu to vent. When

Lu started talking about going to the house again, Jody stopped her with a few whispered words.

"I'm sorry he hurt you," she said simply.

Lu stopped in her tracks. She sighed heavily and sat down.

"How did you know?" she asked.

"I know you. And unfortunately, I know him. It makes sense and explains a lot about why you're so determined to have Anna with us. I don't know how exactly, but I've always known."

Jody watched Lu's internal struggle with what she said. When tears threatened to fall, she pulled her into a solid embrace.

Through sobs, Lu added even more distressing news.

"It wasn't just him. My father too, before he died. Something about that house changes the men who live there. They become so hateful and evil," Lu pulled back from the embrace and looked Jody in the eye. "And don't say it."

Jody knew exactly what Lu didn't want her to say that day, and she wondered if things were really different now. Would Lu tell Anna everything, including what she herself all but admitted that day, when she said the word 'evil'? The house was full of evil. The curse was real.

Jody shivered remembering the figure she saw that day so long ago in the Marshall's living room. The boy who looked so angry and pointed at her. She'd never told Lu, but she saw him again, the night of the fire, hanging from the tree in front of the house. He looked exactly the same as the first time, wearing tattered, bloody clothes with the rope around his neck. The only difference was that the second time, the house burned behind him and the other end of the rope was tied around a tree branch. He saw her too. And pointed his finger at her again.

Jody knew Lu had her secrets, but Jody had a few of her own as well. She also had information that Anna needed to hear. Lu wasn't the only one keeping Anna in the dark.

Chapter 12
1983

Anna sat in her room, trying to read but mostly trying to stay quiet. Occasionally she heard things breaking downstairs, so she knew Mama and Daddy were fighting.

She hugged Ruthie and felt a little comfort in knowing that she wasn't alone.

Nonetheless, she jumped, and her stomach tightened when David yelled, "Anna! Get down here now!"

Anna crept down the stairs and peered around the corner. She was ready to run if Ruthie said to.

David saw Anna hesitate.

"Get over here now," he said. He and Mama were sitting on the couch. Mama was pacing.

"What happened?" Anna asked.

"Don't talk back!" Daddy snapped.

Anna thought she didn't talk back because no one had said anything, so what was there to talk back to? She didn't say it out loud though.

"I work hard, and when I'm off, I expect to be able to rest. Not have to deal with your crap," Mama snarled.

Anna looked from one parent to the other and waited quietly.

"Well?" Mama exploded after a few seconds. Anna wasn't sure what she was supposed to say.

She went with what felt safe, "I'm sorry?"

Daddy jumped in as though she hadn't said anything.

"Your school called again, and she answered before she realized it was them. We gotta get that caller ID thing so we can know who's calling. What if someone called about business? Because of you, they'd have gotten a busy signal," he said.

Anna debated. Her six-year-old mind was much smarter and quicker than her parents and there were so many things she could say, even wanted to say, but she knew it would only get her in more trouble. She could sense Ruthie telling her to be quiet and not say anything, just get out of there as soon as possible. She shook her head, trying to find words while her parents stared at her.

Finally, she asked, "Did they say what they needed?"

"Who?" Mama demanded.

Anna took a small breath and said, "The school. Why did they call?"

"Yeah. You running up a lunch tab there. I don't know where they get off charging kids for food. You can't eat there no more," Mama finished.

Anna thought quickly. Ruthie was very clearly telling her to be quiet, but Anna wanted to say just one more thing. She shook her head again, trying to knock Ruthie from her mind so she could find the words she wanted. Just before she spoke, a crash sounded from the kitchen. Everyone jumped.

"Now what did you break?" Mama snarled at Anna.

Anna ignored the question and plunged ahead with what she was planning to say.

"If you would sign that paper they keep sending home, I would be able to eat for free," she blurted.

Her parents looked at her with their mouths hanging open. Despite Ruthie's insistent warnings and her father's red sputtering face, she went on.

"It's just a stupid signature. It would take a second and this wouldn't be a problem. Why can't you just-"

The back of a hand flew across her cheek. She stumbled backward, trying to regain her balance, arms spinning in the air.

Run!

Ruthie wanted her to run, and she immediately obeyed. She bolted up the stairs to her room and listened carefully. She heard her parents screaming, and she heard a few loud crashes. But the one thing she feared the most, she didn't hear. She didn't hear footsteps climbing up the staircase.

Anna debated running up the second set of stairs to the attic. It wasn't likely they would climb up to her room and even less likely they would climb to the attic. She continued to listen closely until she was convinced she was safe. Soon they would forget about her and turn their anger toward each other. She crawled into her closet, shaken and scared, as the sounds of a war downstairs escalated. She wanted Ruthie, but she wanted to hide too. She was alone in the closet and pulled the door closed. Ruthie would never go into the closet with her.

The sounds of glass exploding and loud voices saying hateful things continued for an hour, then everything finally went quiet. Anna dozed off and on until she jumped awake. Cold chills ran over her entire body when she realized what woke her.

Daddy had opened her closet door and was standing there watching her. He looked strange and scary. Anna was certain Mama had run off again and that's the only reason it was quiet. She did that sometimes when they fought really bad. And when that happened, Daddy would start drinking and maybe even have to give himself a shot. He said it was for anxiety. Anna really hoped she never had anxiety because she hated shots.

David swayed and blinked repeatedly. He had one hand on

the doorknob and was using it to steady himself, but the door kept moving and so he kept listing to one side. Anna remained curled up in her closet. Her eyes, large and unblinking, focused on her father. She wondered what to do if he should fall or even worse, if he were to go to sleep in her room. She didn't want to sleep in the same room as him.

Finally, he reached down and grabbed her arm. As groggy as he looked, his grip was firm, and he hurt her. He began to cry as he picked Anna up and carried her to the bed. She wondered if she should try to comfort him. She had never seen him cry before and wasn't sure what to do. They sat like that for several minutes. Anna, held captive in his embrace as he cried. Tears and snot ran from his face down Anna's shoulder and back.

She started to squirm. The hug was going on way too long, and she didn't want to comfort him any longer. He smelled awful. She recognized the mix of chewing tobacco and his cheap beer on his breath. There was another smell too. It smelled like the doctor's office or when Ms. Canter cleaned the classroom with bleach. She wanted to get away more than anything, but he held her tightly and wouldn't let go.

When David started rocking back and forth against her leg, Ruthie swept into Anna's mind and took over. Anna did exactly what Ruthie said.

Go away, Anna. Go away.

Chapter 13
1983

The next day Anna woke up sore and tired. She slowly rolled over and pulled her knees to her chest. Between her legs burned and ached. She felt something sticky between her thighs and gently touched herself. She looked at the blood on her fingers. Her first thought was that maybe she had her period. She wasn't sure exactly what that was or what it meant. She knew that it happened to girls like the one in the commercial with the gymnast doing splits. Mama always said girls get weird stuff going on between their legs. Could that be why she was so achy?

She looked at herself and took inventory. More sore spots on her arms and legs. If the school was ever to call, it would be today for sure. And then Mama would be even angrier about them calling, and she and Daddy would fight and this whole thing might happen all over again.

She vaguely wondered if Mama was even home. Sometimes she stayed gone for a day or two after a fight like they had. She thought about faking sick, but it was worse to be at home than at school. Especially if Daddy was still here and awake. Anna sighed heavily and pulled herself out of bed. She fought waves of nausea and weakness. Maybe she really was sick.

She slowly crept down the stairs, holding tight to the railing to keep from stumbling. Her legs were wobbly. The house had one bathroom. It was on the first floor, tucked under the stairs. If Mama or Daddy was in there, she would have to go outside. Not her favorite thing to do, but it was better than having to pee all the way to school. She knew she wouldn't make it without an accident. And she had to do something about the blood. Thankfully the bathroom was empty, and the house was quiet. Anna cleaned up as best she could and stuffed a little wad of toilet paper in her panties to soak up any more blood that might leak out.

She climbed back upstairs and stood in her room, torn between the overwhelming desire to crawl back into bed and the equally overwhelming desire to leave the house. Finally, she made a decision. Despite the heat, she pulled on a long-sleeved shirt and her old jeans that always fit too baggy. They covered enough.

No one was downstairs when she left the house to catch the school bus. As she walked to the bus stop, she practiced what to say just in case she was sent to the nurse again. Ruthie helped her find the words to explain why she looked so tired. She would be okay just as long as the school didn't call again. That's what started everything in the first place.

The ride to school was bumpy and miserable. Every pothole sent waves of nausea and pain through her body. By the time she got to school, she was pale and sweaty. She didn't even make it into the building before the teacher at the front door steered her straight to the school nurse.

"I feel okay," she said feebly as Nurse Janey guided her to a cot and covered her with a blanket.

She tried to remember the words she practiced earlier. How was she going to convince this nice lady that nothing was wrong with her? She laid on the cot and closed her eyes straining to hear who Nurse Janey was talking to and what she was saying.

Anna wanted to explain, but her throat hurt, and her mouth was so dry. She couldn't make her brain work or make her mouth say words. And the few times she did remember what she wanted to say, she would fall into a disturbed sleep right before she could get the words out.

She woke up when she heard someone say Aunt Lu's name. She listened carefully and finally relaxed when she realized that's who they were calling. She finally fell into a deep sleep.

When she woke up next, she was in a large white bed. It was comfortable but unfamiliar. She looked at her arm. There was a tube taped to her. She didn't like it and immediately tried to pull it out.

Anna felt Aunt Jody's warm hand gently move her hand away from the IV.

"Leave it alone," she said softly. "It's helping you to rest."

Anna closed her eyes and fell back asleep.

"I'm her aunt," Lu said when the nurse asked if she was Anna's mother.

"Can we reach a parent?" she asked.

Lu and Jody looked at each other.

"We've tried," Lu said. "They aren't answering their phone."

A police officer walked up with Lori and overheard them.

"I'll go get her," he offered.

"That would be-" Jody started, but Lu cut her off.

"No, thanks. I'll go," she said.

Jody grabbed her arm and turned her so they faced each other.

"No, let the police," she said intensely.

Lu shook her head and pulled her arm free from Jody's grasp.

"What should I tell the parents?" Lu asked the nurse.

"Try to find the mother," the nurse said. "We need to do a sexual assault forensic examination. We don't want to wait much longer."

Lu looked at Jody. Tears were flowing freely from her eyes.

"Don't," was all Lu heard before she turned and walked deliberately down the hallway. That was all she needed to hear. It was happening. There was no way David would get out of it this time.

Lu made it to the house in record time. She hit her brakes hard and sent gravel and dirt flying into the air. She slammed the car into park and flung the door open. Leaving the car running, she stomped to the front porch.

"David! You son of a bitch! I know you're in there!" Lu called out as she side-stepped the weak planks and began banging on the door.

Amber opened the door the second after Lu banged on it. She blocked the entrance as she yawned and rubbed her eyes. She wore old leggings with holes in them. The threadbare shirt she wore confirmed that she wasn't wearing a bra.

"What are you yelling at him about now?" she demanded.

Lu hated this woman more than anything. Her relationship with David was awful anyway, and it had been for as long as she could remember, but when he started seeing Amber, it got even worse. Amber was hateful and manipulative. She wasn't raised in this house. She knew better.

"Do you even know your daughter is in the hospital? Why aren't you answering your phone?" she spat.

David sidled up behind Amber and Lu poked her finger at him.

"What did you do to her?" she demanded.

David rolled his eyes and turned on his heel. He trundled back into the house. Lu tried to follow him, but Amber started to close the door on her. Lu stuck her foot in the doorway.

"Your daughter is in the hospital," she repeated loudly. "Do you even care? I know you are abusing her," Lu yelled through the partially open door. "I know you use drugs. And I know you had sex with her David! David!" she screamed his name again and again.

Lu could see Amber's narrowed eyes glaring at her through the space where Lu's foot was wedged. Amber turned to her side and put her shoulder into the door. She threw her weight behind it. Lu's foot was throbbing, and she tried to pull it out, but it was held fast between the door and the jamb.

Frantic and angry, Lu felt like she was losing her mind. She kept hearing Jody's voice telling her to let the police handle it and for a brief moment she wished she'd listened.

She alternately pulled her leg and pushed the door, trying to get Amber's significant weight to let up. Suddenly the door flew open. Lu registered Amber flailing backwards at the same time she windmilled her arms to keep her own balance. Stepping back, her foot hit the sweet spot on the porch, and she crashed through the hole. She was stuck with one leg in the hole and the other stuck out at an awkward angle. As she worked to get her free leg under her so she could stand, she saw the shotgun.

Lu screwed up her strength and courage. She managed to pull her foot free and scrambled upright. She faced her brother on the porch and stared into his eyes.

"Everyone knows, David. The police will be here any minute," she said quietly. "And you better hope they get to you before I do."

He didn't say anything to her. He didn't need to. She knew the look in his eyes better than anyone, even Amber or Anna. And she knew what he was capable of. She turned her back to him and walked to her car. As soon as she closed the door, she began shaking and crying. She wanted to talk to Jody more than anything. She forced herself to drive slowly until she found a payphone. She called the hospital and asked for Anna's room.

Jody answered on the first ring.

"Come back," she said gently.

Lu continued to cry, hiccups and hysteria threatening to take over.

"Breathe," Jody said. "In and out, slowly."

Lu obeyed and began to calm down.

"Any better?" Jody asked.

Lu sniffled and dug in her bag for a tissue to blow her nose.

"Yes," she said before she blew. "I'm coming now."

"Good. Drive safely," Jody said before hanging up.

Jody turned to the small group who faced her. While she talked to Lu, Lori had managed to get Amber on the phone. She swore she was on her way to the hospital right now, but that was a lie. Lu would have said something if Amber had passed her on the road.

It was evident Anna had been raped, but there were still questions as to who had done it. Based on Lori's report, the police were willing to pick up David. At the very least, for questioning. They wanted Amber to be out of the house first though. She had a history of becoming belligerent towards the police.

Jody wanted Lu to be here, with her, before any of that happened. If Lu saw the police heading towards the house, she was likely to turn around and follow them. Lu had a good head start though, so if she drove straight to the hospital, she would make it easily before Amber. And possibly be off the two-lane road before the police passed on their way to the house.

The nurse motioned for Jody and Lori to join her.

"Someone hurt her pretty badly," she whispered.

"Did she say anything?" Jody asked.

The nurse shook her head. "She's slept through most of it. I didn't have the heart to wake her for all of that."

"Good," Jody said.

Relief and then dread passed through her body when she saw Lu running down the hallway. She shared a look with Lori and could tell she felt the same way.

"How is she?" Lu asked, out of breath and sweaty.

"Resting," Lori said.

Lu looked at Jody hard.

"You know what I'm asking."

"I'm sorry," Jody said.

Lori was crying silently and trying to hide her tears. When Jody looked at her, her own tears began to fall.

Lu swung to face Lori. She pointed her finger at her.

"Figure something out," she said. She turned on her heel and stomped into Anna's room. She sat on the edge of the bed and held Anna's hand gently.

Jody and Lori watched her.

"I'm sorry," Jody began.

"No, you have nothing to be sorry for. I failed her. This is on me," Lori said.

"No, it's not. You did all you could. I know that," Jody reached for Lori's hand. "Lu knows that too. She's angry at herself and at David, not you."

Lori opened her mouth to thank Jody for her kind words but was interrupted by the sound of flip flops slapping the polished floor of the hospital. Amber was bustling down the hallway, carrying a tissue that she used to dab the sweat from her forehead. Her hair was wild and unbrushed. Her face looked like she had just woken up and her clothes were mismatched and dirty. It looked like she attempted to put makeup on but only drew black lines around her eyes. She had lipstick on her teeth.

She glared at Lori and Jody as she swept past them and into Anna's room. Lori and Jody followed on her heels.

Amber stopped short and glared at Lu. Lu stood and took several quick steps toward Amber. Jody just managed to squeeze herself between Amber and Lu and gently nudged Lu several paces back. She reached for Lu's hand and held it tightly.

Amber looked like a trapped animal. She glared at everyone in the room and then narrowed her sites on the nurse who was busy checking on Anna. She emitted a low wail that startled the nurse who turned abruptly to see what the strange noise was. Amber used her shoulder and hip to push the nurse away from Anna's bed. She stood where the nurse was and began shaking Anna's shoulders to wake her. When Anna finally opened her eyes, Amber was the first thing she saw. She blinked rapidly several times and then scooted to the other side of the bed. She rolled over so her back was toward her mother.

"She's still asleep," the nurse said trying to smooth out the awkward moment.

"No, she hates her mother," Lu said.

Jody watched the nurse gather her paperwork while keeping a thin smile on her face. She watched her walk out of Anna's room and straight to the nurse's station where she picked up a phone. Jody could see her gesturing emphatically to whoever was on the other end. She was pretty sure security would be showing up soon.

She turned back to the drama playing out in the room. Amber stood looking at Anna's back with narrowed eyes. Her arms were crossed over her chest.

"I'm going down for a donut and coffee," she said to no one in particular.

"Wait," Lori said. "We have to talk first. The police are on the way to arrest David. Did you know what was going on in your own house?"

Amber shook her head sadly. "No. It wasn't David. Anna is fine. She probably just fell down or something. You know the house is cursed."

Lu sprang across the room and grabbed Amber. She pushed her to the wall and leaned in hard, pinning her shoulders. Jody moved quickly and put a hand on Lu's arm, but she wasn't going to stop her this time.

Lu's face was inches away from Amber's.

"Anna was raped. By David. He didn't have to hurt her," she hissed. "He had a choice."

Amber pulled herself free from Lu. She looked at the women standing around her. Without another word, she turned and left Anna's room.

Amber walked as fast as she could towards the elevator. Her mind spun wildly. If David were arrested, she would lose his check and then how would she buy things? And if she lost Anna too, would she even be able to stay in the house? She knew she had to show that she was a good mother to keep Anna with her. But she also had to save David and keep him from being arrested. And she needed to do both things in order to protect herself.

When she stepped off the elevator, she found a payphone and called David to tell him what was going on. She needed to tell him to hide. He answered but talked in a low voice. He had heard them coming, he told her, and hid in the secret room in the cellar. He waited till they left and then came out when the coast was clear.

"When are you coming back?" he asked.

Amber didn't know how to answer that question. She was pretty sure they wouldn't let her bring Anna home if he was still there. But she also couldn't tell him to leave. It was his house after all.

She finally told him she would be there soon, then hung up.

She got a cup of coffee and sat in a corner of the cafe, thinking. She needed both of them there but was pretty sure that wouldn't work out. They believed David did this. Amber figured it was probably true. After the fight they had, he most likely went on a bender. That stuff he used made him even crazier than usual and he was probably out of his mind. At least it didn't happen very often.

Her thoughts were interrupted when Lori sat down opposite her.

"They are discharging Anna," she said without preamble. "David did this to her, and you have to protect her. You have to keep him away and if he does show up, you have to call the police. Do you understand?" Lori demanded an answer.

"But we can stay in the house, right?" Amber asked.

Lori's hands were folded together and resting on the tabletop. Amber noted that her knuckles were turning white.

"Is David at the house?" she asked.

"No. I made him leave," Amber said quickly. Maybe this would work if he just stayed hidden in the house.

"As long as David stays away, it looks like they'll let you take her," she said. "Apparently someone important likes you. I don't agree with it, but it's not my decision. But do you understand what is happening? Do you see how badly David hurt her? You should want to keep him away and take care of Anna. Do you understand taking care of Anna is your only priority?"

Amber never answered Lori. Instead she stood and gathered her things. She walked to the elevator with Lori following behind.

The ride in the elevator was uncomfortable and quiet.

Amber stared at the floor, still trying to find a solution to what she was beginning to think of as the "Lori problem."

When they exited the elevator, Amber decided to be the best mother any of them had ever seen. She walked to Anna's room quickly. Anna was awake and sitting up. Lu and Jody were standing on either side of the bed, holding her hands and talking to her. Amber took in the scene quickly and then made her way to the bedside. The nurse was there too, and a police officer was just coming through the door.

Amber smiled and held out her hand to the officer.

"Mrs. Marshall," she said.

He took her hand and shook it quickly.

"Can I speak to you for a moment, privately?" he asked.

Amber smiled coyly and said he could do whatever he liked to her, privately.

"Um, I guess we can talk here," he said, clearing his throat. "We didn't find David at the house. Do you know where he is?"

Amber shook her head.

"I've no idea. I kicked him out before I came here," she said. She tried to sound innocent and sincere.

The officer went on to inform Amber that since they couldn't find David at the house and Amber insisted he was gone, Anna was being released to her.

"And if we find that he is at the house, or that you know where he is and aren't telling us, you will be in trouble too, Mrs. Marshall. Do you fully understand me?" he asked.

Amber rolled her eyes. She looked at Anna and Lu. Lu was bent over Anna and they were whispering. Amber wondered what they were saying about her.

"She's my daughter, and we will be fine," she said to the officer. "I'll take good care of her."

She smiled sickeningly sweet and waved her hands to shoo the group away.

Lu kissed Anna's forehead and whispered to her again.

Amber knew she couldn't keep calm much longer. She just knew they were talking about her, and it was infuriating. All she wanted was to get Anna out of there and go home. She and David had to get this figured out quick.

"Go and let me tend to my daughter," she said. Then she turned to the officer. "Please, let me have some time with my little girl. Can you make them leave?" She asked, jerking her head towards Lu and Jody.

The officer nodded. Amber watched as he uncomfortably herded the small group into the hallway. They stood in a line. Still watching and judging her.

"Hug your Mama," Amber hissed as she bent to tuck a stray hair behind Anna's ear.

Anna lifted a hand and patted Amber's arm. Amber smiled and looked over her shoulder to make sure everyone saw what Anna did.

"She loves her Mama," she said loud enough for the group in the hall to hear.

"She doesn't even have a booster seat," Jody mumbled.

The orderly arrived. Amber gathered Anna into her arms and tried to hold her. The orderly tried to help her place Anna in the wheelchair, but she refused to let her go. She almost dropped her a few times before finally thrusting her into the chair. Anna cried out in pain, but Amber ignored her.

"Let's go," she said.

As the orderly rolled Anna out of the room, they passed by Lori, Jody and Lu who stood solemnly watching the spectacle. Lu and Jody stepped forward to give Anna one last hug, but as they passed, Amber put herself between them and the wheelchair. They couldn't get by her.

They made their way down the hall. Amber chatting happily with the orderly who was still trying to make sure Anna was comfortable.

"It won't last," she heard Lu's voice ring down the hallway.

"You won't be able to keep up this act. You'll screw it up, and I will be there!"

Amber didn't say anything. She followed the orderly into the elevator and positioned herself just behind him and Anna.

As the doors began to close, she looked at Lu, raised her middle finger, and smiled.

Chapter 14
1983

The phone was ringing when Lori got to her desk Friday morning. She spent a restless night worried about Anna. Several times she almost talked herself into driving to the house to check on her. The only thing that stopped her was knowing it wouldn't be safe to go alone. She suspected David was still there.

That morning she was up early. She went straight to the office to have some coffee and wait for Jack. Being the biggest guy in the office, he offered to go with her to the Marshall's house. She gratefully accepted, knowing she would feel much safer with Jack tagging along.

She scooped the receiver up.

"Lori Jamieson speaking."

"I'm leaving the house now," Jack said. "Wait for me."

Lori tried to distract herself with paperwork, but she wasn't able to concentrate on any of it. Mostly she paced the small office, waiting for the sound of Jack's car. When she finally heard him, she raced through the door and jumped into the passenger seat.

"Let's go," she said.

Amber sat up. She thought she heard something and listened carefully. Yes, she heard correctly. Someone was coming. She heard tires crunching on the gravel and knew a car would be stopping in front of the house any second. The driver was moving fast.

"Damn," Amber muttered.

"What is it?" David asked through a mouthful of chewing tobacco.

They were both up early today. David came up from his hiding place in the cellar late last night and neither one slept much. They were awake now, lying in bed watching TV.

"She's back. Quick, you need to hide," she said.

Amber swung her legs from the bed and pulled her sweatpants on. She ran her hand through her greasy, lank hair as she jammed her feet into her flip-flops. She looked in the mirror. Black eyeliner was smeared down her face. She rubbed it away as best she could and applied even more around her eyes, believing it helped.

She glanced at David, still lying in bed.

"You need to hide," she moved between him and the TV and stood with her hand on her hip.

He smiled, but he didn't move. Amber felt a wave of panic begin at her feet and rush through the top of her head. What if it was the police, and they somehow knew he was here? Would she lose the house? What would she do if they took him away? It was infuriating how David believed he would never be in any trouble.

She tried one more time.

"Hide!" she screamed louder and meaner.

"Look at you," he laughed at Amber. "Putting on your makeup, trying to be all fancy." He rolled to his side and opened the bedside table where he kept an emergency joint. He put it in his mouth and began looking for a lighter.

"Got a light?" he asked Amber.

"Oh my god!" she screamed. "Give me that!"

She reached for the joint, but David was quicker and rolled across the bed, still laughing. Amber spoke between clenched teeth.

"Laugh at me all you want. But when that woman takes Anna, and then the police show up and take you, you'll be sorry," she hissed.

"You'll be sorry," he said, mocking her.

Amber saw no other option. She would go answer the door and whatever happened, she would just have to deal with it. Maybe it was nobody, and she would just run them off. She started towards the door when she heard David. He was standing up now, straightening his own clothes.

"This is my house. I'm not going anywhere, and I'm done hiding. Let whoever it is in. They can't do nothing to me," he said.

Amber nodded silently. At least he was out of the bed. She walked towards the door with David close behind. Before she reached for the doorknob, David shoved her to the side and flung the door open himself.

"What?" he barked.

Amber saw it was Lori Jamieson. Her eyes were wide and a little wild. Behind her was a large man. He stood with his arms crossed over his barrel chest.

"You can't be here," she declared.

"No, you can't be here," David said, and he started to close the door.

Jack was too fast though and before David realized what happened, he threw his shoulder into the door forcing it wide open. David lost his balance and staggered back while Lori and Jack darted inside.

Amber still stood where he had shoved her aside in the hallway. She reached out to steady David, but he jerked away from her.

"You have to kick him out," Lori shouted. "You said you made him leave!"

"I did," Amber said. "Then he came back. Who the hell is this?" Jack was standing in the doorway, legs spread, and arms crossed over his chest again.

"It doesn't matter. Amber, he can't be here," Lori tried again.

Amber thought quickly. Her eyes landed on the baseball bat that lived in the corner of the hallway.

"You're not coming in today. I'm busy and don't have time for you," she said. She reached for the bat.

Jack stepped in front of Lori.

"Let's go," he said over his shoulder.

"No, wait," Lori said. She stayed behind Jack but moved so she could see Amber clearly.

She took a long breath and tried to reason with Amber.

"I'm sorry that I had to come unannounced today. I know you don't like that, and really, neither do I. When we left the hospital, we were under the assumption David wasn't staying here any longer. Obviously, he's here," her words hung in the air.

Something crashed in the back of the house. It sounded like a glass shattered. Amber looked at David and then looked upstairs. She was sure Anna was still in bed.

"So, I need Anna," Lori said, ignoring the crash. "I'll take her to her aunt until all of this gets resolved. She'll be safe and with family."

"Well, it's not quite that simple," David began. Another crash stopped him from saying more to Lori.

He looked at Amber.

"What the hell?"

She shrugged her shoulders and glanced upstairs again. She was going to have to go look for that kid before she broke everything in the house.

"I know you don't want the police coming here. Please let

me take Anna and you guys can go on with your lives. You don't really want her," Lori spoke quickly from behind Jack. Her only priority was getting Anna out of there no matter what.

"No!" Amber screamed. She made a threatening move towards Jack and Lori. She held the bat raised over her shoulder. Before she could swing, David stepped forward and grabbed the bat from Amber's hand.

"That's it. I'm done with all of you. If you try to take that girl away, there will be a whole mess of trouble for you. You get what I'm saying?"

His voice had dropped to a menacing low growl. Now he was holding the bat over his shoulder as though ready to swing.

"You need to git, now," he pointed at Lori. "And take your bodyguard with you."

Then he turned on Amber. "And you need to stop that kid from breaking everything."

"Come on," Jack said. "Let's go."

"But, Anna," Lori began.

"We'll come back for her. Come on," Jack said. He began to nudge Lori towards the door.

"Fine," Lori said. "But I am coming back and I'm bringing the police."

Amber watched until the car was out of sight and the last bit of dust had settled. She knew they would be back soon and have the police with them. There wasn't much time, and she still had to convince David to hide. She also had to find out what that kid was doing, creeping around the house breaking things. She closed the door and was startled to see Anna standing at the top of the stairs.

"Go back to bed," she said.

Chapter 15
2019

A bhay walked into his office and flopped down into his chair. He spun the chair around twice then stopped. He was still worried about Anna's panic attack. He had driven Lily to school and left Anna at home, still sleeping.

It wasn't a coincidence that she was hearing Ruthie at the same time he received the letter. He fingered the edge of the envelope and then pulled the paper out. He studied it closely. It was addressed to Anna and to Lu but mailed to their Knoxville address. Normally he would never have opened mail addressed to Anna, and definitely not mail addressed to Lu. But this one was unique and something about it made him tuck it away in his pocket until he could open it privately, in his office and away from Anna.

The return address was Jonesboro. That's what really caught his attention. It could only be about one thing. The remains of the house that his wife and her aunt still owned. As far as he knew, it was still there, just rotting and falling down. He should have given the letter to Anna immediately, but with the panic attack and everything else, he knew it wasn't the right time. Abhay shook his head.

"That's enough justifying," he mumbled. He opened the letter and began to read it.

It was on the official town letterhead and explained that the town was undergoing a major renovation. Old houses and buildings were being restored and there was a strong emphasis on authenticity. They wanted to be historically accurate in every way. Apparently, they were also interested in the Marshall's house.

The letter went on to explain some of the family history. Abhay knew most of it. The house was built in 1860. Abhay wasn't sure if the Marshalls owned it then. But he knew, and the letter confirmed, that the Marshall family had lived there for generations, well over one hundred years. Apparently, it could be an historical landmark if they could rebuild it like it was. A lot of the original wood survived and even though it had been exposed for decades, it was in surprisingly good shape. The town wanted to buy the house, and the land, and turn it back into its original state. It used to be a trading post. He figured it would be more like a general store nowadays.

Abhay knew that neither Lu nor Anna wanted anything to do with the house. But they didn't want to sell it either. The few times they discussed selling, both had argued that a Marshall had owned it since it was first built. All additions or renovations were done by Marshalls. Despite the recent events in the family's history, they viewed the house as part of them and part of their family.

Abhay had witnessed first-hand the trauma related to that house and knew how it still affected his wife. He couldn't do anything about the past, but he was determined to protect her future.

He made his decision and called the number on the letter. He would make the hour and a half drive to visit the house, and then he would get back to them.

Anna and Lu would have to be involved for anything to be legal and official, but Abhay would visit the house alone and see what it looked like before he even spoke to Anna, or Lu, about it. He didn't want to upset either of them if there wasn't a reason to. He doubted they would sell anyway, but you never knew. And the town was offering a decent sum. Plus, it would be nice to not have to pay property taxes any longer on a place they did nothing with.

Thankfully, it was a light day at work, and he cleared his calendar easily. He turned off his location app just in case Anna happened to look for him. He was being paranoid, but he knew she would be very upset and worried if she saw he was in Jonesboro when he was supposed to be at work.

The drive was pleasant. It was a clear, sunny day and there wasn't much traffic on I-40. Highway 81 had even less traffic and he laughed out loud when he realized he didn't see another car on 11-E for miles.

He lost himself in the view. The mountains were nothing new to him. In Knoxville, he had mountain views, and they took regular trips into the Smoky Mountains, just a thirty-minute drive away. But it was different here. There was no mountain view exactly because they were actually in the mountains. It was always a little cooler, a bit more snow in the winter, and always a little greener in the spring. He slowed down as he took Exit 23 and drove into downtown Jonesboro.

He would need to use GPS to find the house. He'd only driven by it once when he was a kid and had no idea how to get there. He enjoyed his drive through the quaint town. They had done an amazing job so far restoring the historic buildings lining Main Street.

Abhay shared Aunt Jody's interest in history and had looked up several items about the town over the years. He was especially curious to see the Chester Inn. It was the oldest building in downtown Jonesboro and was built in 1797 by William Chester. It housed three presidents back in the day: Andrew Jackson, Andrew Johnson and James K. Polk. Abhay even learned of the local story that while staying there,

Andrew Jackson scandalized the area when he helped fight one of Jonesboro's many fires in only his nightshirt. The building had served as a tavern, an inn, a library, apartments and was now a museum and visitor's center. He smiled at the freshly painted building. The balcony and the arches looked especially good.

He turned onto the street across from the Inn and parked behind Mauk's Pharmacy. It felt strange starting up his laptop in the middle of the quaint old town. Even stranger when he easily found a Wi-Fi signal.

He did a search for the town, looking for information specifically about how his wife's family fit in. He looked up several dates to refresh his memory on the timeline. The house was built less than a hundred years after Tennessee became a state which was one year before the Civil War began. Most likely his wife's ancestors did not own slaves, despite being wealthy, because a large part of the area was pro-Union. Another confirmation came when he found that the Marshalls helped support The Emancipator in 1819. This was a paper dedicated to abolishing slavery. Apparently, they were also involved in helping to bring the railroad to Jonesboro in 1849.

The last positive piece of information he could find was a small notice about the Marshalls going to the World's Fair in Chicago in June of 1893. The story promised another article with an interview because the family wanted to share all they saw and bring the culture and education back to their small town.

Abhay couldn't find the much-promised follow-up story anywhere. He assumed they returned home, but it seemed like they disappeared completely. He couldn't even find death notices for the family. He shuddered to think they were all buried on the land near the house. He made a mental note to check around for headstones or some sort of grave markers when he got there.

As he scrolled through time, he finally reached the 1920s

and once again, the Marshalls made the news. The most inter-esting being some notices of the Marshall family involved in moonshine bootlegging in 1920 during prohibition. Apparently, the family continued the business for a few decades because another notice from 1945 showed an old photograph of a Marshall family member being arrested for running moonshine.

Abhay snapped his laptop closed and rubbed his eyes. He punched the address into his GPS. He was about eight minutes from the house.

He started the car and pulled out slowly, looking around intently. His tires bumped over the cobblestones on the side-walk as he navigated to the road. Abhay was lost in thought.

How could a family that began so prominent and integral to the growth and establishment of this town, a family who committed time and money to see it flourish, suddenly turn into an actual burden on the town?

Within a few minutes, he found himself on a narrow country road. He enjoyed the full width of the road as his Maxima hugged the curves and corners. Abhay tried to imagine what it was like to run bootleg moonshine over this road. Even though the road was in pretty bad shape, he knew it had to have been worse back in 1920.

Probably all dirt, he thought.

His GPS told him his turn was coming up, so he slowed down. After driving for another five minutes, he realized he'd missed the turn. A quick five-point turn in the middle of the road and he was heading back the way he'd come. He went even slower this time, scanning the side of the road for any hint of a driveway connection. He realized he'd missed his turn again when he recognized a giant red barn with "See Rock City" painted on the side. Cursing under his breath, he alter-nated between drive and reverse as he turned around in the middle of the road again.

He put his window down this time and hung his head

outside to watch even more closely for any sign of a turn. He was in luck. Weeds had taken over the edge of the road, but just past them, he could make out ruts in the dirt. He turned off the main road and followed the dirt path, his tires sinking alarmingly at times, pitching the car to dizzying angles.

Abhay was so focused on not bottoming out his car, he almost ran right up to what was left of the old porch. He braked quickly and looked up.

He had been led to believe the house burned to the ground and always assumed there was nothing left. He was wrong.

The overall shape of the house remained. Granted, the wooden frame was blackened, and the clapboard siding was gone in a few places. It looked more like a giant had taken a large bite out of the side of the house, but the other side was mostly okay.

Abhay parked next to an old tree that stood in the front of the house. It looked dead but wasn't rotting or decomposing. All the other trees around it had leaves and the apple trees had fruit, but this poor thing only had thick bare branches, sticking out at all angles.

He turned his attention from the tree and made a mental inventory of the things he wanted to check out. First, a cemetery. He scanned the yard and the land just beyond as he looked for any sign of a burial plot. It was hard to tell with the weeds so high, but he thought he saw a flat area just past the barn that might have served as a family plot.

Thankful that he thought to bring boots, he changed shoes quickly and grabbed his bottle of water and cellphone. A quick walk to the back of the house confirmed that this was indeed a family burial plot of some kind. Based on what was left of a few headstones and indentations in the earth, he guessed seven or eight people were buried there. He could make out the remains of a rusted wrought iron fence a short distance away. He walked to it and began pulling away weeds and grass. He saw a small stone in the middle and used his hands to clear away dirt and weeds. It seemed to have served as a headstone at one time. Abhay stood and looked around him. He could imagine small graves surrounding him and shivered at the thought of the children buried right under his feet.

He turned his attention back to the house. The side that stood looked sturdy enough. It was clapboard so paint had almost peeled off completely. The exposed wood made up the majority of the house.

Yellow pine? He wondered to himself.

He picked his way around to the burned-out shell of the house and peered in. He could see the floor and debated walking in, at least part way. He knew there was a cellar below, and while he would have loved to explore the cellar, he didn't want to get there by crashing through the weakened floorboards.

He continued around the house and found another area that appeared to be cut away rather than burned. He assumed the firefighters went into the blaze from this direction and had removed some of the siding on the house. Peering in through this area, he pulled his cellphone from his pocket. It was dark. The roof was intact and there were no windows. Turning on his cellphone flashlight, he shone the light into the void.

Abhay jumped and dropped the phone.

"What the...?" he mumbled to himself. He picked up the phone and turned it again toward the ruins. He saw what had startled him. It looked like a closet that was open. The tattered remains of a shirt hung listlessly. He told himself that's what he just saw, although a small part of his mind could swear he'd seen a young boy.

He briefly wondered if squatters were living there. He didn't think so. The house was mostly empty and very quiet. He also wondered if teenagers from the area were using the house for parties, but he didn't find any discarded bottles or beer cans, no cigarette butts, no graffiti. Nothing to support that theory.

Abhay continued his investigation around the perimeter until he found an entrance to the side of the house. Not the kitchen and not the front door, he wasn't sure what this door was used for. Nonetheless, it was still closed, and it looked undamaged, so he opened it cautiously. It wasn't even locked. The door opened into a sort of storage room that was mostly empty. A wooden chair lay on its side in the middle of the room. An old stone fireplace stood proudly in the center. The room opened onto a hallway, so Abhay crept through to peer down the hall with his cellphone flashlight.

A shadow flicked past him and again he jumped, this time letting out a yelp.

"I'm screaming like a little girl," he said to himself. "Come on, get a grip," he continued to mumble. "Animals are probably living here, cats or something, raccoons, birds."

Despite being thin and healthy, he was sweating profusely. His heart beat fast, and he struggled to breathe. It was hot and stuffy this far into the house. He knew it was time to turn back, but he was torn. His curiosity, and something else, pulled him deeper into the house.

Anna and Lu always used the same word to describe the feeling in the house, oppressive. He understood what they meant now. He felt it too. Some of it was because of the fire, sure, that would make any house feel creepy. But this was something extra, something sinister.

Abhay laughed out loud at himself.

"You're losing it, dude," he said. Pulling himself out of the trance he'd fallen into, he turned to leave.

This time he saw it clearly. A boy, thin and lanky, wearing torn and tattered pants and a shirt that was covered in something dark.

Blood, passed through Abhay's mind. He froze, staring in stunned silence at the boy who stared back. It felt like minutes but was only a few seconds, and then the boy moved in jerky, quick movements down the hall and into another room. Abhay followed him.

"Hey!" he called. "Hey, wait up! I just want to talk. You're not in trouble."

He made his way toward where the boy disappeared and cautiously entered the room. The light in here was a little bit better, but he still held his phone up out of habit.

He scanned the room with the light but couldn't find the boy.

"How did you get out?"

Abhay walked the edges of the room, looking for an exit. There was none. Instead he found an old pocketknife laying on the floor. Abhay loved woodworking so without a thought he picked up the knife and turned to leave. As he made his way through the house, he continued to look for the boy, whipping himself around randomly to look behind him in case he was being followed.

Once back in the bright sunshine, Abhay took a long breath. The sun and the fresh air helped him forget about the boy he saw. He told himself he imagined it and laughed at how spooked he was.

He forced himself to be rational and began scanning his surroundings for some good wood. He thought it would be a nice memento to carve something for Anna from the house, especially if they ended up selling it.

Abhay lucked into a loose piece of yellow pine propped against the wall right next to the door he had entered.

"How did I miss you?" he said, picking up the wood and brushing it off.

Aside from some rough places on the outside, it was in good shape. He could easily sand it down and was sure he'd find quality wood hiding underneath. Abhay smiled to himself thinking about his project.

He walked back to his car and sat inside with the air conditioning cranked up as high as it would go. He looked at the knife carefully. The outside was made from antler and he could barely make out the "Case XX" mark on the tang.

"Wow," he said under his breath. He knew he held an antique. "Maybe late 1800s?" he mused.

He was determined to get it cleaned up and in good working order and as soon as that was done, he planned to use it.

His drive back to Knoxville was a blur of thoughts about the wood and the knife. He completely forgot about the purpose of his visit and of selling the house. He also forgot about the boy he saw. The only thing in his mind now was the knife, the wood, and his new project.

Chapter 16
1983

J *ust breathe*, Lori thought.

Her head felt like lead, and she couldn't lift it. She lay on her side, vaguely aware that blood streamed across her face and dripped off her nose. She watched the puddle growing larger under her head. She closed her eyes and tried to make her mind work.

She went to work that morning. Jack picked her up and they went to the Marshall's house. Yes, she remembered that clearly. They left and called the police from the office. Why was she here though?

Lori couldn't make sense of what had happened. She remembered sitting in her office, waiting for an officer to return her call. She would go with them to the house. The police would take David, and she would take Anna.

Lori heard a phone ringing.

Yes, she thought. *That's what happened*.

Her phone rang. She answered thinking it was the police, but static made it almost impossible to hear. She listened to what sounded like a child's voice on the other end.

"Anna? Anna is that you?" Lori asked.

Through the static and pops, Lori could barely make out what the caller was saying. She heard one word clearly though.

Help.

"Anna! Anna is that you? Anna!" Lori shouted into the phone as panic rose.

She dropped the phone and looked around desperately, praying someone else was still at the office. Everyone was out making their own visits. She was the only case manager there. She glanced down the hall where the administrative assistant sat. She was a small, older woman. No help at all.

There was no time to waste. She told herself the police were on their way, so even if she got there first, surely they would be right behind her. She scribbled a quick note on her calendar. Date, time, and location, then she rushed to her car.

Now she was curled into a ball, bleeding all over the Marshall's front hallway. She opened one eye. The other was almost swollen shut. Two sets of bare feet stood in front of her, just beyond the spread of blood. She closed her good eye and blacked out.

Amber looked at David. He was smiling.

"Good job," he said. "Now what?"

Amber was shaking. She looked at the bloody hair that was embedded in the end of the bat. She shook her head slowly and looked at David.

"Finish up," he demanded.

Amber shook her head.

"You telling me no?" he asked.

"The police," she managed to whisper. "They'll come."

"Let 'em," David stated. "They won't find anything. Especially if you'll get your ass in gear. Come on. I'll help you clean up your mess."

Amber watched as David began to roll Lori Jamieson up

in the rug that she was bleeding all over. She watched Lori try to fight, weakly moving her hands. She even tried to speak a few times. Then she got very quiet.

"Are you going to answer that?" Amber asked. The ringing of the phone was jarring her nerves.

"Might be the police," he surmised. He was breathless from the effort of rolling the rug. "You really want me to answer it?"

"No," Amber said. She watched him while the phone continued to ring.

"She's still alive," Amber whispered.

"Then finish it," David said.

Amber shook her head. She couldn't believe she had done that, but she didn't have a choice. Lori Jamieson came back too soon. Amber knew she would be back and probably have the police with her, and she had a plan to hide David. She was getting good at listening carefully for sounds of cars on their driveway. The problem was she was so tired that she fell asleep. She only woke up because she heard David talking to someone.

She knew immediately that the woman was already in the house. Amber had slept through everything and never had a chance to put her plan into action. Jamieson threatened everything Amber had. Without thinking, she grabbed the baseball bat that was still sitting where she left it last time. She only swung once, but that was enough.

Now she watched, fascinated by David's precision and deliberate movements. The normally lazy man she lived with slowly came alive. It was as though he was in his natural element and was doing what he was made for.

When he got Lori rolled up, he dragged the rug to the door.

"Come on, open the door for me. Dammit! Wake up Amber," he grunted at his wife.

Amber made herself move. Between the two of them, they

managed to get Lori's body into the back of their truck and covered her with an old tarp. They went back into the house and stood in the kitchen, sweating and tired.

"Now what?" Amber asked. The phone had finally stopped ringing, and she was able to think clearly.

"Get me a beer," David said.

Amber reached into the refrigerator and pulled out one of David's cheap cans. She popped the top and set it on the counter. The moment she removed her hand, the can tipped over and foamy beer ran down the face of the cabinets.

Amber jumped and set the can upright quickly and looked at David. She braced herself for his flood of anger towards her. Instead, he reached for the can and took a long sip. Then he belched.

"Let's go dump the body," he said, matter-of-factly.

"Do I have to come?" Amber asked. Her voice shook, and it was hard to breathe.

"'Do I have to come?'" David repeated in his mocking way. "You did this, so yeah, you have to come. Grab the keys and come on. You drive," he ordered.

"Anna?" Amber said. She wasn't sure why she said Anna's name or what she thought David would do differently.

"She's fine," he said over his shoulder. "Come on."

The old, beat up Ford turned over after three tries. Amber sat on the driver's side of the bench seat. She adjusted the torn vinyl under her leg so it wouldn't poke her and then rolled her window down. Through the cracks in the windshield, she scanned the surroundings.

"Relax," David said. "No one saw us."

"You're right. No one saw us," Amber agreed.

But they were both wrong.

Chapter 17
2019

Anna woke up and stretched. She flipped over and read the time on her cell phone. It was ten in the morning. She listened carefully to the sounds in the house. There weren't any. She was off today, and it was the first time she'd been alone in the house since the day after her panic attack. She wanted to keep Lily home with her, but Abhay insisted she needed to rest. He'd been very cross with her the last few days, and she wasn't sure why. She didn't argue with him and he drove Lily to school.

She crawled from the bed and shuffled to the bathroom. Her image in the mirror startled her. Peering closer, she ran her finger down the wrinkles on the side of her eyes. She had dark spots under her eyes and something else. She looked closer.

"Grey?" she said, more as a question than a statement. "Ugh," she turned from the mirror.

She shuffled into the kitchen to find a full pot of coffee, still warm, sitting on the counter with her favorite mug sitting next to it. She smiled at Abhay's thoughtfulness. It was a comforting gesture after the night before. They seldom argued, but his mood was so bad, she was frustrated with him and pressed him for answers about his attitude.

He blew up at her and stomped around grumbling something about all the women in his life not leaving him alone. Anna responded by reminding him of all the time he spent lately, outside, alone, carving whatever it was he was working on. For the last several days, every spare moment he had was spent whittling and carving.

Anna thought back to the day of her panic attack, about a week ago. That was the last day things were really normal. His anger started the next night. She tried to think of what could have triggered his mood, but the only thing she could think of was that he was angry about Ruthie. He knew about Ruthie though and the night she told him, he was as supportive as always.

Anna sighed and put her coffee cup down. She glanced at the clock on the stove and stood. She had an appointment in two hours and needed to get ready. She had two days off this week for a therapy appointment and a follow-up with her doctor. She didn't really need two days off for these appointments, but she enjoyed the freedom and the time to relax.

———

"I'm worried about Abhay," Anna told Dr. Rhodes two hours later. "He's been acting so strange lately."

"How is he acting?" Dr. Rhodes asked as she settled into her chair and pulled a fresh notebook from her stack.

Anna watched her doctor while a tug of war took place in her mind. She wanted to help Abhay and was almost certain he was upset because of Ruthie. If she didn't tell Dr. Rhodes about Ruthie, she couldn't help Abhay. She kept her face neutral and as casually as she could, she told Dr. Rhodes she was hearing Ruthie again, and she had told Abhay about it.

"But it's only been for a little while," she added quickly.

She wanted to soften the lie, and she wasn't ready to admit that Ruthie never really went away.

Dr. Rhodes nodded solemnly.

"This doesn't surprise me," she said. "How does it make you feel, hearing Ruthie?"

"Not much of anything. It's like she never left," Anna added in a flat tone.

"And Abhay? How do you believe this has affected him?" Dr. Rhodes asked.

"I think that's why he's acting so strange. Like, he's angry with me for Ruthie," Anna said.

"We need to talk about Ruthie," Dr. Rhodes put her notebook down and looked intently at Anna. "This is big."

"I know, I know," Anna said. She didn't want to talk about Ruthie at all. She wanted to talk about Abhay and how he was acting. Anna reminded herself that this was new information for Dr. Rhodes, while she herself had been living with Ruthie all this time. It wasn't a big deal to her, but it was to Dr. Rhodes. Anna smiled. She would explain it away like she had done for most of her life.

"Okay, I'll be honest. I have heard Ruthie off and on for years. I didn't tell anyone because I knew everyone would get upset. Ruthie hasn't bothered me or upset me or even impacted me at all. I just kept it to myself. I started to tell you so many times. I'm sorry," she finished.

Dr. Rhodes only nodded.

"Can we talk about Abhay first? And then I'll tell you everything?" Anna tried to negotiate. She could tell Dr. Rhodes was not pleased that she withheld this information.

"Okay then. Tell me how he's been acting. What's he doing?" Dr. Rhodes asked.

Anna let out a sigh of relief. She was more comfortable talking about Abhay than about Ruthie.

"His temper is short. He seems irritated by everything.

He's even different with Lily. And-" Anna stopped talking and grabbed her head with both hands.

"Anna, what's wrong?" Dr. Rhodes asked.

Ruthie had begun raging in Anna's mind. It sounded like she was banging pots and pans. The thudding completely disrupted her thoughts. Anna held her hands over her ears and closed her eyes trying to will Ruthie to stop. She was so loud.

Dr. Rhodes dropped her notebooks and sprung to Anna's side. She tried to pull Anna's hands from her head.

"Look at me, Anna," she said.

Anna opened her eyes slowly and looked at her through stray strands of hair. The thunder in her head stopped.

"What just happened?" Dr. Rhodes asked.

"Ruthie," Anna said. "She doesn't want me to talk to you about this stuff."

"She controls what you say?" Dr. Rhodes asked.

"No. It's hard to explain," Anna said. She sat up straight and tried to compose herself.

Dr. Rhodes was watching her closely.

"I'm okay," she said. "It's over."

"Is this how she usually talks to you? Have you been dealing with this all these years and never said anything?" Dr. Rhodes asked.

"No, not at all. It's been ages since she's done something like that, and she's never done it when I've been with you," Anna explained. "Usually she just puts words into my mind, or ideas. Nothing that loud or sudden."

"Is she putting into your mind right now? You were telling me about Abhay and how he's been acting."

"She's telling me I should run. Not say anything else. Like, she thinks I'm in danger," Anna said.

Dr. Rhodes sat back next to Anna. She was quiet for a long time, and Anna began to wonder what was going through her mind. This was more than she had ever admitted to anyone, even Abhay. Was the doctor thinking she was crazy? Would she want her to go to the hospital? Medication? Anna was beginning to panic even more in the silence that continued. She tried to calm herself with deep breathing but was only making herself hyperventilate.

"Relax," Dr. Rhodes said. "There's nothing to be upset about. I'm only thinking."

She looked at Anna and smiled. Anna tried to smile back.

"I think we can safely assume Ruthie is not an imaginary friend, correct? Whatever she is, she has more influence in your life than I think you want," Dr. Rhodes said.

"Can you help me?" she asked in a small voice.

"Yes," she said. "Can you come back tomorrow?"

One of the best things about being a psychiatrist, Deborah Rhodes thought as she watched Anna leave her office, is always having someone to talk to. She went to her partner's office and knocked.

"Got a minute?" she asked.

"Sure," George looked up from his paperwork. "Did we have a session scheduled? I'm sorry, did I forget?" he started shuffling papers around and looked ashamed. George was forgetful but this time he didn't forget anything.

"No, George. You're fine. I just finished with Anna, and I wanted to talk to you about her. Is this a good time?"

George leaned back and folded his hands into a pyramid in front of his face. This was his usual posture when meeting with clients. It bugged Deborah a little but not enough to keep her away. Especially after the session she just had.

"What's going on?" he asked.

"It's not good George. She's hearing voices again. She said it started a little while ago, but as you know, I've suspected it never went away," she said.

"And has she admitted that it's not an imaginary friend?" he smiled slightly as he asked.

"Yes," Deborah said.

"Well, it's good that she's admitted it, right?" he asked.

"Maybe. After talking to her today, I'm starting to wonder about Dissociative Identity Disorder. The way she talked about this voice and how it stops her from saying certain things. It's very concerning," Deborah said.

"Can you tell me more?" he asked.

"It was hard to get much out of her. She wasn't very clear. I get the impression whatever it is blocks her memories. And that it controls her. She made the comment that it didn't want her telling me certain things," Deborah shook her head slowly.

"How can I help?" George offered.

"I'm not sure," she said as the door buzzed. "Your next patient is here."

"So I noticed," George said standing. "When do you see her again?"

"Tomorrow."

"Let's talk this evening. We can put our minds together and see if we can make some sense of this. We'll get a treatment plan started," he said.

Deborah thanked him and left through another door to preserve his patient's confidentiality.

She wandered the long hallway back to her own office, deep in thought. Like others before her, Deborah had long wondered if it was Anna who actually caused the fire that killed her parents. She firmly believed the Anna she knows now could never have done it. And she found it hard to believe Anna at six could have done it. That any child could do something like that.

Deborah sighed in frustration as she opened her office door. She stood in front of her bookcase, scanning her library, hoping to find a book that would miraculously provide all the answers. She found one that looked promising and returned to her desk.

The vase of fresh flowers that usually sat on her desk now lay on its side. Water had pooled in the middle of her desk pad. Deborah realized it was there just in time before she ruined the book.

"How did that happen?" she mumbled to herself. She lifted the desk pad and let water stream into the trash can then set it on its side on the floor to dry. She had a few napkins in her desk drawer that took care of what was left.

Anna's stories of getting into trouble as a child when things were knocked over or broken flashed through her mind.

"Coincidence," she muttered as she brusquely rubbed the goosebumps on her arms.

Chapter 18
2019

"Where have you been?" Abhay asked.

Anna and Lily burst through the door laughing and giggling. Anna's arms were full of packages, and Lily carried a small bag.

"We have dinner," Lily said. She held her package up for Abhay to see as she twirled through the kitchen. Anna smiled. The elastic that held Lily's long, brown hair slipped further down her ponytail and she tripped over her own feet, losing a sandal in the process.

Anna laughed out loud and looked at Abhay. He was watching Lily too, but he didn't smile.

Anna put the packages down and paused. Something was wrong.

"Lily, go change clothes and color in your room. I'll call you when it's time to eat," Anna said.

"Ok, Momma," she sang. She picked up her shoe and hugged Anna.

"I had fun," she said.

"Me, too," Anna smiled. "Now scoot."

When she was sure Lily was out of earshot, Anna turned to Abhay.

"What's going on?" she asked.

"Why weren't you at work?"

"I took the day off, remember? I had an appointment with Dr. Rhodes and tomorrow I have an appointment with the doctor. You even suggested I take a few days off after the panic attack. Plus, The Aunts are coming tomorrow, and I want to get the house ready," she explained.

"Why didn't you check in?" he asked.

Anna paused before answering. Her stomach knotted as the tension in the room rose. She felt like she did as a child. Trying to find an answer to a question that she shouldn't have been asked. It didn't help that Ruthie was whispering to her again. Twice in one day was too much. Anna shook her head to clear the thoughts and images.

"I didn't know I had to check in," she said.

"When you're out with my daughter, spending my money, you need to check in," he said.

The voice in Anna's head was clear now.

Run. Go away.

Anna bit her tongue and stood her ground. She was an adult now. This was her house too. She had a choice. She could ignore his mood and tell him where they were. It was simple. She had a difficult session with Dr. Rhodes and wanted to have some fun. She picked up Lily early, and they went shopping. It was a much-needed time with her daughter and had lifted her spirits immensely. She would leave out the part about Ruthie though.

Instead, she chose not to say anything. She turned on her heel and left the kitchen. As she changed clothes, she decided she would talk to Dr. Rhodes about all of this tomorrow. She wouldn't escalate the situation and would avoid Abhay for the rest of the evening.

"Come on, Lily. Let's eat," she called.

Lily bounded from her room and followed Anna back into the kitchen.

"Where's Daddy?" she asked.

Anna scanned the room.

"I don't know," she said. "Let's not worry about Daddy right now. He's busy. Here, start eating."

She and Lily jumped when they heard a loud crash from outside.

"What was that?" Lily asked. Her eyes were big and round.

"I'll check. Stay here and keep eating."

Anna peered through the window and saw Abhay. He was pacing back and forth, waving his arms as though arguing with someone. On the ground lay what was left of a six pack. The bottles were broken, and foamy rivers of craft beer ran everywhere.

Anna turned back to Lily.

"Daddy tried to balance his drink on the railing and it fell. It's okay. Just some broken glass," she said.

While Anna and Lily continued with their nightly routine, Abhay stayed on the porch. Every time Anna peeked out the window he was in the same position, head bent, elbows on his knees, slowly whittling. Anna looked one more time before she went to bed.

The next morning, he was still there. The only difference from the night before was the growing pile of shavings beneath Abhay and the increasing intensity of Ruthie's warnings.

Chapter 19
2019

"What has she said about 'fire'?" Dr. Rhodes asked.

"Nothing specific. It's just the word imprinted on my mind with her little voice whispering, warning me. It's hard to explain," Anna said.

"Has Abhay hurt you or Lily in any way?" Dr. Rhodes asked.

"No! Of course not! He would never," Anna stated emphatically. She truly believed that about the old Abhay. But, really, she didn't know about this new one. She wasn't completely sure she trusted him.

"It's really just his temper, his mood, I guess. He's unapproachable. Doesn't want to talk. He sulks? I think that's a good word to describe it. And he's dark. Like a dark cloud hanging over him," Anna said. "He's...unpredictable."

"Okay, first I'll remind you of boundaries. You aren't responsible for his mood. As long as he doesn't hurt either of you, or anyone, this is an issue he will need to work through. He's been here before so maybe another appointment would be in order. It's likely he has a lot on his mind and knowing him and your family through the years, I know he is probably worried about you. But for the rest of our time, I'd like to talk about you and Ruthie," Dr. Rhodes said, then added, "and the fire."

Anna nodded. That was the whole reason for this appointment. To talk about what happened yesterday. She knew it was important, but she was over it all and so tired of talking about the same old things. She really wanted to figure out Abhay.

"The fire I don't remember?" Anna asked. The words came out more aggressively than she intended.

Dr. Rhodes continued, unfazed by Anna's tone.

"You said you and Abhay invited your aunts to visit this weekend. Is that still on?" she asked.

"Yes, I suppose so," Anna said.

"This would be a good time to ask them to fill in some blanks. Especially now with so many things coming up for you," Dr. Rhodes said.

"I've tried before," Anna said. "Aunt Lu doesn't like to talk about it, Aunt Jody thinks the house is haunted, and Ruthie tries to stop me any time I ask too many questions."

"How does she stop you? Like yesterday?"

Anna sat back on the couch and brushed away a tear.

"No, yesterday was different. Usually it's much more subtle. It's not like she makes me unable to speak. Or that she physically does something to me. It's more a feeling. An overwhelming dread, fear, that makes my body tired, and my thoughts aren't clear. I forget words and can't concentrate on anything. Then I get distracted and it all goes away. Sometimes Ruthie is the reason but sometimes, I think I use her as an excuse to stay safe in my bubble," Anna said.

Dr. Rhodes nodded.

"I blame Ruthie because I think she is the reason I can't remember things. I suppose the fear I have from not being able to remember the fire has leaked into everything in my life. I'm afraid and so I always blame Ruthie for holding me back. She's been a constant through it all," Anna said.

She had never said this before. Fear was the key. She lived

in fear and blamed Ruthie. She sat for a moment and let that thought sink in. Ruthie was a friend when she was young, but now, as an adult, Ruthie, and the fear she represented, was holding her back from finding the truth. Ruthie was an old story that no longer served her. She didn't need to be protected from anything any longer. Last night proved that. She handled the feelings that came up with Abhay without Ruthie's help. Anna felt a weight lift from her shoulders as this realization began to sink in.

"What are you thinking?" Dr. Rhodes asked.

"I've always blamed Ruthie for everything wrong in my life. But I'm the one who is responsible, right? I have a choice. I can control what I think and what I do, not Ruthie. I did it last night," she said.

"Who do you think Ruthie is," Dr. Rhodes asked.

"When I was younger, as you know, I called her an imaginary friend. But after the fire, they worried I was ill. They thought it was strange that I heard a voice, so I pretended that I didn't hear her any longer. She became my secret," she said.

"Is she still an imaginary friend?" Dr. Rhodes asked.

"Sort of. But adults don't have imaginary friends, do we? And we certainly don't hear them talking to us. Aunt Jody has a theory," Anna said. "She thinks the house is haunted."

"Do you think Ruthie is a ghost? Or a spirit?" Dr. Rhodes asked.

"Maybe," Anna cringed. Was she admitting to believing in ghosts now? She kept talking, trying to explain herself.

"I believe in energy. I think when someone dies their energy is still around. Since energy can't be created or destroyed, then where does it go when we die?" she asked.

"Well, when we think about all the people who died in your house over the generations it makes sense that they left some sort of energy behind. I think that's reasonable," Dr. Rhodes said. "Do you believe Ruthie is this energy?"

Anna sat back and let her body sink into the cushions of

the couch. She pulled her legs up and tucked them under her. She closed her eyes and rubbed them with her finger and thumb.

"Give me a minute, okay?" she asked.

"Take your time," Dr. Rhodes said. She began jotting notes as Anna drifted into deep thought.

Anna reflected on all the strange things that happened in her house. The strange sounds, scratch marks in the closet, moaning sounds in the cellar, crying in the attic, and things randomly breaking. It was an unspoken rule in her house that no one talked about it and they definitely didn't talk to outsiders about it. Jody was the only person from outside the family to scratch the surface of what happened. And she believed in ghosts and spirits.

"I don't know who Ruthie is. An imaginary friend? A spirit, energy, a ghost?" she said with a smile. "The things that happened in the house were just another unspoken generational secret. We were so isolated until I lived with The Aunts, I didn't know anything was unusual about my house or my family. Looking back, I was a weird kid," she said.

Dr. Rhodes nodded along.

"What do you think?" Anna asked. "And I know your response is going to be that what you think isn't what matters. I need to figure out what I think. But really, I'm at a loss. What does your gut say?"

"Well, of course, I can't say if your house was haunted or not. And I can't say why your family avoided outsiders. But I do see a pattern from talking to you all these years. I am comfortable saying something was not right in your home when you were little. There was obvious dysfunction. We know there was neglect. We also know they had a temper. And we know there was physical abuse. We also know your parents abused dangerous drugs while you were in the house," Dr. Rhodes ticked off each point on her fingers.

"Is it possible you ingested hallucinogens somehow?" she asked.

Anna shook her head and then shrugged.

"Just because you don't remember details doesn't mean you weren't impacted by your parents' actions. In fact, the exact opposite. The fact that you don't remember leads me to believe your mind is protecting you from trauma. And Ruthie is your mind's way of doing that," Dr. Rhodes said.

"There is a lot more to the story than what I know," Anna agreed.

Before she could stop herself, Anna blurted out the one thing that she questioned every day of her life. The one thing that made her wonder what kind of person she was deep down. The one thing that made her think she was truly ill.

"Do you think I started the fire that killed my parents?" she asked.

"No, Anna. I do not think you killed your parents. You were too young to even think that way. Yes, they were not kind people, and you were certainly mistreated, but no, you don't have that in you," Dr. Rhodes said.

"And Ruthie?" Anna asked.

"I don't know. Obviously, she protected you as a child, and still does to some extent. It could be your mind created her and just hasn't been able to let her go yet. You've heard from her lately and you've been under a lot of stress. Starting with seeing DCS visit a child at work. And with Abhay acting strangely. A lot has happened lately," Dr. Rhodes said.

"I don't want her protection any more though," Anna said. "It's not protection when it stops me from doing things I care about, when it stops me from remembering things I want to know."

"We will keep working together and figure it all out. In the meantime, please be kind to yourself. The more frustrated you get with yourself because you can't snap your fingers and make it better, the harder it will be to work through it all. It will take time. Just the fire in itself is a lot to process. All the other stuff just complicates things even more," Dr. Rhodes finished.

As she drove home, Anna thought about telling Abhay what Dr. Rhodes said about Ruthie protecting her. She was excited to tell him that finally, she was ready to hear the entire truth. To ask Aunt Lu and Aunt Jody the hard questions about her childhood and to face the answers no matter what they might be. Anna was ready to be healthy, and the only person in the world she wanted to talk to about it was Abhay. She smiled as she turned on the radio and sang along.

She hoped this would clear the air, and he would feel better too. Maybe they could get back to normal, but this time, without Ruthie in her head.

Chapter 20
2019

Anna arrived home to find Abhay, sitting on the couch in the dark. She hesitated for a second, then flicked on the lights. She'd spent the drive home getting more and more excited about the decision she made in therapy and was convinced this was the news that would snap Abhay out of his weird mood.

"You'll never guess. I had a major realization today. I'm ready to hear it all, Abhay. I want to know why I have these strange feelings, and I want to know once and for all if I had anything to do with the fire. I feel so confident and kind of excited," Anna admitted.

She ignored his lack of response and began straightening up the living room as she talked.

"Abhay? Where is Lily?" she asked.

"Friend's house," he answered.

"Oh," Anna paused. "Which friend?"

"Down the street, um, Jessie."

Anna stopped cleaning and looked at him. His eyes were closed.

"Did she invite her over? I'm wondering because, well, you

138

know, The Aunts are coming today. I know they will want to see her," Anna said.

Abhay sighed heavily and turned to face Anna.

"What's with the interrogation? Can't I take my daughter to a friend without being questioned?" he said forcefully.

Anna deflated.

"We had plans tonight. The whole family, Lily and The Aunts, you and me. You changed it without saying anything. I'm allowed to ask why," Anna stated.

She could feel Ruthie hovering near her, trying to put words in her mind. Anna pushed back. Ruthie wasn't going to control this. Anna was in charge. When it came to Lily, she drew the line.

She watched Abhay. She wanted an answer even if it led to a fight. He had a small wooden disk in his hand that he alternated between rubbing with his thumb and flipping through his fingers.

"Is that what you worked on last night?" she asked.

"Yeah," he said.

"Abhay, what's wrong? You've not been yourself lately. Is something going on? I'm worried about you."

Abhay still didn't make eye contact. He rolled his eyes and sighed. Silently, Anna sat on the couch beside him and turned towards him.

"Look, we've always been able to talk. We've always been honest with each other. Have I done something? Are you mad at me? Are you sick? Is it work? Tell me, please."

Abhay finally looked at her, his eyes brimming with tears. Anna immediately reached for him and pulled him into an embrace. He allowed her to hug him, and she felt him relax slightly. Tears dripped down his cheek and pooled on her shoulder.

"What? What is so bad? What is it?" she mumbled.

Abhay pulled back slowly and looked her in the eyes.

"I wish I knew," he said quietly. "I'm just so irritated. So angry and frustrated. I want to hit something. I feel like- I feel rage inside me. I don't trust myself. That's why I took Lily to her friend. I wanted her away from me. I would never ever hurt her," he added quickly. "That's why I wanted to be alone."

When he finished talking, he looked back at his carving. Anna watched him flip it through his fingers. As he did, she could see his shoulders getting tense again, rising up towards his ears. She wanted to reach out and hold his hand, but the mood was shifting.

"It's because of Ruthie," she said.

"What?"

"You started feeling this way when I had the panic attack and told you about hearing Ruthie. Is it her? Are you angry at me because of her? Be honest," she added.

"No! I'm not angry because of her. I hate the situation, but I'm angry, frustrated at everything, everyone. There's not any one reason. I don't know where this feeling is coming from, and I don't want to talk about it anymore," Abhay said.

Anna was about to answer when the doorbell rang. Before she could stand, they heard the sound of keys in the lock.

"Hello?"

"We're here!"

"Where's Lily?"

It sounded like a bulldozer was coming through their front door. Abhay looked at Anna and smiled.

"Ah! The Aunts are here!" he said.

Relief flooded her body as Anna caught a glimpse of the real Abhay. She felt like maybe everything would be okay after all.

"Let's talk some more later," she whispered. She reached for his hand, but in a split second, his smile faded, and he jerked his hand away from her. He dropped the disk into his pocket and hurried to the hallway, turning his back to Anna.

"Hi! How was the drive?" he asked a little too loudly.

Anna shook off her feelings and greeted The Aunts with a smile and a hug.

"Lily is with a friend tonight. She doesn't even know you're here or she never would have gone," Anna explained, covering for Abhay. "It's probably for the best though. I want to talk to you both tonight. Serious stuff from therapy, I'm afraid."

Lu looked at Jody and smiled.

"Perfect! We want to talk to you too," she said.

Chapter 21
1983

"Wha' was that?" Amber slurred.

She thought she heard something break. She opened her eyes and looked around without moving her throbbing head. The day came back to her in slow motion. She remembered driving the woman's body far into the woods where no one would ever find her. They dug a hole and put her in it. Then they covered the spot with leaves and branches. The police never showed up either. That was an unexpected gift.

Amber thought about the other gift they had. They gave the woman's car to their dealer in exchange for pretty much anything they wanted in order to make the day disappear forever. They were in the clear and they celebrated all night.

David slept with his head back and his mouth open. She untied the elastic from his upper arm and shook him gently. This was her man. And sure, he had a lot of issues and was a real pain sometimes. But he was mostly fun to party with; he had this house and some money. And he took care of her. Today proved that. He was the quick thinker when it came to getting rid of the body, and it was his idea to trade busy body bitch's car for drugs. Let someone else deal with it while they relaxed.

She nudged David and whispered, "Let's go to bed."

David mumbled something as he reached for a cigarette. He lit it as Amber stood, pausing to get her balance. She picked up the jar of moonshine they had bought that night. Then she took David's hand and helped him get his balance too. He took the Mason jar from her. He gathered his pack of cigarettes and lighter and followed close behind her.

When they reached the bed, David flopped down. Ashes scattered over the bed, and moonshine sloshed close to the lip of the jar.

"Hey, be careful," Amber said. "Don't smoke in bed. You might start a fire."

"You jus' worry 'bout you," he mumbled.

"Here, let me help." She adjusted the jar into his armpit so it was wedged between the side of his chest and his upper arm. Amber patted him on the head then moved to her side of the bed.

She lay down beside him.

"Put your cigarette out," she said. Then she passed out.

Anna woke to a growling stomach. She was thirsty too and her sore muscles needed to move. She listened carefully and then decided it was time. She thought her parents were asleep, and she could sneak to the kitchen undetected.

She carried her doll tightly pressed to her chest as she crept down the stairs, avoiding the creaky ones, and peeked around the corner. She could see Mama helping Daddy stand up.

Anna pressed herself back into the darkness and stroked her doll's matted hair. She made herself small and quiet as a mouse. Maybe they were going to bed, and they wouldn't see her. Anna prayed nothing would fall or break and draw their attention back to her. Her feet were cold on the hardwood floor. She vaguely wondered what happened to the rug that was always there.

She peeked around the corner again and watched as Mama and Daddy stumbled and staggered like drunk teenagers to their room, giggling and holding onto each other. Anna's nose wrinkled at the strange chemical smell that told her they would sleep for at least a full day, maybe two.

As soon as they disappeared into their room, Anna crept to the outside of their open door, her small body pressed against the wall. She could hear them talking and again, waited patiently. It wasn't long before she heard them both snoring. Now she could walk to the kitchen undetected and have whatever she wanted.

Her bare feet padded quietly past the room and around the corner to the kitchen. She pressed her palms flat on the countertop, jumped, and swung a leg up in one smooth motion. She pulled herself up and balanced on her knees. Anna was high enough now to open the cabinet door and be able to feel around the lowest shelf. She found a plastic bag of bread shoved to the back. Inside were two regular slices and both end pieces.

She hated the ends. Anna pulled the regular slices out. She wadded up the bag and stashed it back into the cabinet. She hopped off the counter and then carefully opened the refrigerator door. There was an orange-yellow package of cheese that wasn't completely closed. She pulled the dried crusty cheese from the edge of a slice and put the rest on the bread. Then she pulled the crust off the bread.

She found a dirty glass sitting within reach and ran it under a thin stream of water to rinse it then she filled it with tap water. The whole time took longer than she liked, but she didn't want the tap to make the rumbling noise it made when turned on full blast. She was patient. When her glass was full, she crept from the kitchen, sandwich and water in hand. Her doll was securely tucked under her arm. She stopped at her parents' room. Curious, she crept through the partially open door and stood at the foot of the bed, watching them sleep.

Anna could smell the smoke from David's cigarette and that other smell too. It made her sick. She chewed thoughtfully as she watched the cigarette in her father's hand. A long ash balanced precariously on the end. Mama always fussed at Daddy for smoking in bed. She said it could start a fire and burn the whole house down. Anna was pretty sure Mama would be really angry if she was awake right now and saw this.

The open Mason jar was on its side now. Moonshine seeped into the bed, soaking the sheets and David's shirt. His hand slipped off his chest and the barely lit cigarette rested on the soaked bed.

Anna's stomach growled. She was still hungry. Even though only the ends of the loaf were left, she decided she would make do and walked back to the kitchen. She didn't worry about being quiet this time. She was certain they wouldn't wake up.

That night, Anna sat in the front yard, eating a sandwich made with the ends of the loaf. She held her doll and shivered despite the heat of the fire behind her.

Chapter 22
2019

Jody looked around the room at her family. With the exception of Lily, all of her favorite people were right here. She pulled a fuzzy blanket over her legs and snuggled into an oversized chair, balancing her wine glass on her knee.

Anna and Lu sat on the couch, both curled into the arms of the sofa with their feet tucked under them. Their wine glasses in hand. Abhay was sitting on the floor, away from everyone. He kept fiddling with a piece of wood and appeared to be pouting about something. He grumbled about breaking things when he was offered wine, so he didn't have anything to drink.

"Abhay, are you feeling okay?" Jody asked.

He didn't answer. Jody looked at Anna and made a questioning face. Anna shrugged.

"Abhay?" she said again.

Abhay looked up and slowly and deliberately made eye contact with each of the women in the room. Then he looked back at his hand and focused on flipping the disk through his fingers. When it got to his pinky, he lost control and it rolled across the room, landing in front of Jody.

She bent to pick it up.

"No! Don't touch it!" Abhay shouted as he sprang across the room.

Jody had already picked it up and immediately dropped it again. She felt the color drain from her face. She was light-headed. She looked at her hand and then at Abhay. He lay sprawled across the floor on his stomach, clutching the carving.

After a few seconds of awkward silence, Lu spoke.

"Jody, are you okay?"

Jody nodded slowly and looked at her hand. It felt very cold.

"You sure?" Lu asked again.

"Yes," Jody whispered.

"Abhay? What is that?" Lu asked.

He didn't answer. He was spread eagle on the floor, face-down, clutching the carving.

"It's a carving he's been working on," Anna explained. "He started it a little while ago. About the time I had the panic attack and started to hear from Ruthie more. I think he's mad at me," Anna said.

As Anna and Lu continued talking, Jody became obsessed with the carving Abhay was still holding. Something about it grabbed her attention. She was determined to get her hands on it again. Although it had hurt her hand, that only made her more curious. She slowly moved to the floor. She set her wine glass on the coffee table and then crawled closer to Abhay.

"Give me the carving."

Anna and Lu stopped talking and looked at Jody. Abhay shook his head slowly.

"I'm not asking, Abhay. Give it to me now," she said.

Without raising his head or saying anything, Abhay opened his hand and let the carving fall out.

Jody grabbed her blanket and used the edge of it to pick up the small piece of wood without touching it. She wrapped it several times and carried the bundle through the back door, into the yard. She set it on a chair. Then she carried the chair into the yard and set it down as far from the house as she could.

Walking back to the house, she could see their silhouettes through the window. They stood in a row, watching her. As soon as she opened the door, they sprang into action. Abhay intently picked carpet fuzz from his shirt and pants while Anna and Lu refilled wine glasses. Everyone acted as though nothing strange had just happened.

Jody closed and locked the door behind her. She took in the charade in front of her and decided it was time to take charge. She resumed her seat in her chair.

"Stop fussing around and sit," she commanded.

Everyone obeyed. Abhay, Anna, and Jody sat on the couch in a row, looking like children waiting to see the principal.

She asked Abhay how he was feeling.

"Better," he said. "Clearer."

He took Anna's hand and kissed the back of it.

"I'm sorry," he said.

Jody nodded then cleared her throat.

"I've been around your family for a very long time. I've seen some things, experienced some things. Even before I met Lu, I had strange experiences. None of you ever wanted to talk about what was obviously going on in that house. It affected all of you, but you denied and avoided. The secrets are a poison that has infected all of us. Secrets about David, about the family history, about the house and the curse on those who lived there. It's time to share those secrets. I think that's why we are all here, in this room. We all have something to tell," she looked pointedly at Anna and Lu, then added, "Including me."

Lu shook her head and opened her mouth to speak. Jody stopped her.

"Lu, I'm right and you know it. If tonight is going to be

about telling the truth, I'll start with my truth. I've kept my mouth shut for decades, watching the trauma and the people I love spin out of control. I talked to Lynda and found out some things I think will help explain all of this," she said.

As she said those last words, Anna reached for her wine glass. Her fingers were just about to touch it when it tipped over and wine spilled and splashed onto her hand.

"Oh!" she said feebly reaching for the glass. Abhay jumped up with a napkin and caught the small stream before it made its way to the floor.

"I must have knocked it over," she said, looking for another napkin.

Jody watched as her loved ones once again ignored what was right in front of them.

"The glass tipped towards you," she said quietly.

"What?" Anna asked.

"The glass. You didn't knock it over. You didn't even touch it. And how could you have knocked it over if it tipped towards you?" Jody said.

She settled back into her chair and held out her glass.

"Abhay, more wine, please."

As he poured, she continued her story.

"Did you ever wonder what led Lynda and me to your house, specifically?" she asked.

"I guess we just assumed because it was so old," Anna said.

"And the rumors," Lu added.

"That is some of it, but there's more," Jody said. "In those six years you lived in that house, Anna, I worried about you every single day. You know a little about my first experience there. You were a tiny baby when I first visited, just born. I talked to your great grandparents, met your mom and dad. Your grandmother aimed a shotgun at me," Jody laughed at the memory as Lu hid her face in her hands.

"That was the least of the problems though. While I was there, I saw something. A form. It was a boy," she said.

Abhay coughed suddenly and made a choking sound.

"Went down wrong," he managed to croak out between coughs.

"Anyway," she continued. "I left the house that day even more curious. But when I met Lu, I stopped looking into it all because she asked me to. Until the night of the fire, anyway."

Jody shivered.

"Remember when Lu and I came to get you? Lu, remember? I stayed in the car? Did you ever wonder why?" she asked.

"Yes, I remember. I was mad at you, you know," Lu said.

"I know. That night I saw something that scared me," Jody said.

She took a deep breath. It was suddenly hard to breathe and felt very warm in the room. She took another deep breath.

"I saw a body hanging from the tree in front of the house. It looked directly at me. It was the same boy I saw the first time I was there. I know why I saw him," she said. Her voice cracked.

Lu jumped from her seat and sat on the edge of Jody's chair. She pulled her close.

"It's okay," she tried to soothe her. "Maybe it was a trick of the light?"

Jody pushed Lu away.

"No! I know the difference. And I saw him twice. I know what I saw," she said, forcefully. She was tired of being dismissed.

"Who was it?" Anna asked. Her voice was small and quiet after Jody's.

"It was William Marshall. He died in 1893, killed by a mob from the town because they discovered the bodies of several young women in the basement of the house. One of his victims was one of our ancestors. That's what Lynda found. It was a relative of ours, Abhay. And our family, the ones who lived then, they took matters into their own hands in their own way. One of them put a curse on the house. That's how our families are connected. The house is evil. William is trapped there because of what one of our ancestors did to him."

Jody looked at the stunned faces looking back at her. Anna had been nodding along as Jody spoke. She could tell Anna was quickly filling in the blanks and had begun answering some of her own questions. Abhay looked stunned.

"I wish I didn't have to tell you that," Jody told Abhay. "We've tried to keep much of this away from you."

"Too late," he admitted. "I saw William, too."

Chapter 23
2019

"When?"
"How?"

"I went there," Abhay answered.

"You went there?"

"What were you thinking?"

"Are you sure you saw William?"

They fired questions at him from all directions. He sat patiently until it was quiet. Then he began.

"I should have told you all. We received a notice from the town. Apparently, the house used to be an historical landmark. An old trading post. They want to buy it and restore it," he said.

"There's nothing left to restore," Lu exclaimed. "It burned to the ground."

"That's what I thought too. So I drove up there to check it out," he said.

"You went there alone? And you didn't tell me?" Anna asked. Her eyes were wide, and she felt goosebumps all over. She shuddered.

"Or me," Lu added.

"Or even me?" Jody asked.

"I didn't tell any of you because of exactly how you are reacting now. I didn't want to upset you, and I hoped to handle everything myself and then be able to just tell everyone at once what was going on, if anything at all," he said.

Abhay looked at his Aunt Jody. He had always dismissed Jody's views and opinions about spirits. She was a good sport about it, but he knew she had every right to say, "I told you so," to all of them. Instead, she was gracious as always.

"I understand," she said. "Go on."

"I went there to see exactly what was left of the house. It's not completely gone. All the original brick is there. The barn is a wreck and falling down from age. It's still there, though. Not burned. The trees and grass are growing. And there's some original wood that was undamaged. I even found some just lying around. It's in good shape. Beautiful yellow pine."

He stopped there. Jody was nodding her head.

"Let me guess. You took some of the wood and brought it back here. That's what is sitting in your backyard right now," she said.

"Yes," he agreed. "I also found this."

Abhay pulled the pocketknife he had found that day from his pocket. He still carried it with him even though it was too dull to use.

"What's that?" Anna asked. They all leaned forward to get a better look.

Abhay told them about seeing the boy in the house and how he tried to follow him.

"I lost the boy, William, but found the knife. Just laying there on the floor. Who knows how long it had been there or who put it there," he said. "I didn't even think about it. I just picked it up and brought it home with the wood I found. And then, I guess I forgot about it all. Until now anyway."

"How did you forget about seeing him?" Anna asked. "I would think you'd remember something like that. And I still can't believe you didn't tell me."

"Says the woman who talks to voices in her head," Abhay shot back with a good-natured smile.

Anna grimaced and stuck her tongue out at him.

"Okay you two. Back on track. When you went to the house, wasn't that about the time of the panic attack? And didn't you tell us Ruthie got more active around that same time?" Jody asked Anna.

"Yes, but how are they related? Why would she come out just because Abhay brought back a knife and wood from the house? I didn't even know he went there!" Anna's voice got higher as she said the last sentence.

Abhay put a comforting hand on Anna's arm and slid it down to her hand which he held tightly.

"Go on, Aunt Jody," he said.

"I know you all don't believe what I believe, but you have to ask yourselves what is going on here. To find out, Abhay actually went to the house and has been clinging to that carving? And look at him now. Since he let go of it, and I moved it out of the house, he's obviously feeling better. More like himself. And whose knife was it? Why was it laying right there for him to find? Does anyone else see a connection?" she asked, exasperated.

"I do, Aunt Jody," Anna added quietly. "I see the connection. All this started the very night after he went there. Didn't it Abhay?"

Abhay counted in his mind and finally said, "Yes. I admit as soon as I touched the wood, I started to feel odd."

"And Ruthie got a lot more active. Is it possible she knew what you were doing? Maybe she was trying to stop you or protect me," Anna said.

"Protect you from what?" Abhay asked. "Me?"

He was looking at the floor, avoiding Anna's gaze.

"Abhay, look at me."

He turned his head slowly. His eyes were brimming with tears.

"I know you would never hurt me, or Lily," she said.

Abhay nodded and smiled. This night was becoming exhausting for them all. Anna closed her eyes and rubbed them hard.

"The problem is that I truly don't know what she's trying to protect me from," Anna said, still rubbing her eyes.

Lu cleared her throat. Anna watched her take a long drink of her wine. She kept the glass in her hand and smiled awkwardly at Jody. Anna looked from one to the other, waiting for the answers to her question.

"There are so many things," Jody began. "Lu, start with Lori."

Lu nodded.

"I suspect there are many things Ruthie feels she needs to protect you from. There's much you don't know and even more that you should know but don't remember. To start with, we never told you what the police suspected happened to Lori," Lu said.

"The police?" Anna asked. As far as she knew, Lori had simply left. As an adult she assumed it was because of the stress of the job, something she could relate to. She always remembered her and thought many times through the years that she would like to try to find her.

"Lori was murdered, Anna. The day of the fire," Lu said.

"Oh no!" Anna covered her mouth with her hand. That explained why she disappeared from Anna's life so abruptly. Especially at a time when Anna needed her. It was difficult news and Anna's heart hurt for Lori. But it was hardly worth Ruthie's activity. It was thirty years ago, and she had moved on without Lori in her life. Yes, it was sad for the young woman, certainly, but Anna mourned the loss of Lori years ago. She just didn't know the loss was because of Lori's murder.

"Do they know what happened?" Anna asked. She looked at both aunts. Jody was unusually quiet sitting with her hands folded in her lap. Aunt Lu was taking mini sips from her wine and stalling.

"Do you remember the rug in the front hallway of the house?" Lu finally asked.

"Yes...that's a strange question," Anna said. She vaguely remembered it only because it was always crooked, and it bothered her.

"They found Lori's body, wrapped in that rug, out in the woods. There was DNA from David and Amber on the rug. Of course, all this came out after the fire," Lu said.

"The last place she was known to be was at your house," Jody added.

"Are you saying my parents killed her?" Anna asked. She was incredulous. "Why would they do that?"

"You still don't remember the days before the fire?" Jody asked carefully.

"No," Anna said.

"Do you remember being in the hospital?" Lu asked.

Anna nodded.

"Do you remember why you were there?"

Anna shook her head. She felt cold in the pit of her stomach, and Ruthie was becoming very active in the back of her mind. She knew she was close to finally getting answers. She pushed Ruthie back.

I need to hear this, she thought. *Let me hear.*

"Why was I in the hospital?" Anna asked. A low rumble began in her head and she silently willed Lu to talk faster.

"When I was a child, in that house, I experienced a lot of the same things you did. Strange sounds, crying, things breaking. The cellar was terrifying. Your great grandparents would punish me by locking me in the cellar. Did you know that?"

Anna shook her head. She felt terrible for her aunt, but she also was ready to find out why she was in the hospital. Ruthie was more insistent now, and the roaring sound was louder. Anna didn't think she could hold her back much longer. This was the closest they had ever gotten to exposing family secrets. She glanced sideways at Abhay. He caught her look and nodded encouragement.

"The worst was when they threw David down there too. He had his own ideas about how to pass the time," Lu looked at Anna carefully. "I think Ruthie has really been protecting you from memories of your father. David hurt you very badly. He's the reason you were in the hospital."

That was it. Ruthie was running wild in Anna's head again. She was louder than she'd ever been before, even louder than at Dr. Rhodes's office. Words and images exploded one after another in Anna's mind. She vainly tried to fight it. She shook her head vigorously, trying to dislodge the voice that drummed in her mind and shut out everything else. She wanted to support her aunt and say something meaningful, but she couldn't form the words.

"No, no, no," she mumbled.

"Anna, what is happening?" Abhay asked. He took Anna by the shoulder and shook her gently.

"What is it?" he asked.

"It's Ruthie," Anna whispered.

"Let's stop," he said to Lu. She agreed readily. Abhay turned back to Anna.

"No, I don't want to stop," she said. "It's my decision, not Ruthie's."

A blaze of heat whooshed through her head. Anna saw and felt white hot flames covering the floor of the room. She covered her eyes again and moaned.

Fire. Run.

"Ruthie!" Abhay said. "We're stopping. Leave her alone now. We're stopping."

Anna heard Abhay talking to Ruthie. A part of her mind registered how strange that was. He'd never done that before. In fact, no one else had ever spoken directly to Ruthie.

Does Ruthie hear him?

In answer to her question, the chaotic dissonance in Anna's mind stopped almost immediately. The silence was complete. Ruthie heard Abhay, and she stopped.

Anna looked around the room. She took in the concern on the faces of those who loved her. This had to stop. She had to get to the truth.

"She's gone," Anna said. "I have a headache."

"You need to rest," Abhay said.

"I want to hear the whole story," Anna said. She was determined not to stop now, not when she was finally close to the truth.

"No," Lu said. "There's plenty of time. I think that's enough for one night."

Abhay agreed and pulled Anna to standing. He put his arm around her and led her down the hallway to their room.

"We'll talk later, honey," Aunt Lu called after her as she made her way down the hall to her bedroom.

"Abhay, I want to keep going," Anna continued to protest.

"Look," he said, sitting on the edge of the bed next to her. "I know. I can't imagine how you are feeling, but let's think about this. You just found out your husband is related to someone who cursed your family a hundred years ago. And that your father hurt you and your aunt. Isn't that enough for one night?"

"No, all it does is raise more questions. I feel like I've gotten a sneak peek and no real answers. Just enough to be more curious, not satisfied. I hate this," she said, exasperated.

Anna flopped on the bed. She closed her eyes and almost immediately fell into a light sleep. She was aware of Abhay pulling a blanket over her and leaving the room.

She dreamed vividly of Ruthie and the house. She saw Ruthie asleep. Someone was leaning over her, whispering.

Ruthie sat up. It was William. She grabbed his arm and begged him to stay. He laughed and told her he had a date.

It was morning. Ruthie woke and climbed out of bed. She made her way through the house, but something was wrong. The air felt strange. Something smelled awful.

Ruthie was looking for William. Calling his name. He answered.

"Don't come down here. I'm coming up."

Ruthie waited for William in the kitchen. He arrived, covered in sweat, bloody hands. Bloody clothes. He walked past Ruthie and went outside to the water pump. He rubbed his hands under the water. He pulled his shirt off and rubbed it under the running water too.

Ruthie slowly walked towards the cellar door. It was still open. She peeked through it and covered her nose. She crept down a few of the rickety steps. A single candle sat on a barrel. Something was in the corner. Ruthie's eyes adjusted to the dimness. Now she could see a young woman. Blood. Dirt. A dress in the corner. Unblinking eyes staring back at her.

Ruthie screamed.

Anna woke up sweating and disoriented. She sat up and immediately heard Ruthie. She told Anna terrible things would happen. Things she wasn't prepared for. She was in danger.

Knock it off, Ruthie, Anna thought. *I just woke up. Leave me alone.*

The voice in her head stopped immediately. Anna was surprised but relieved. She laid back down, closed her eyes and immediately drifted back to sleep. She forgot about the strange dream and Ruthie's warnings.

Chapter 24
2019

As Anna slept, Lu, Jody and Abhay barely spoke to each other. It seemed wrong to talk about the one thing on everyone's mind without Anna there. Jody played on her phone while Lu went for a walk. Abhay sat quietly, dozing off and on.

When Lu returned from her walk, she surveyed the sleepy group.

"Let's all turn in. It was an emotional day," she said. "We could use a good night's sleep."

No one argued with her logic. While Abhay fell asleep quickly next to a gently snoring Anna, Lu and Jody lay awake in the guest room.

"You never actually told her," Jody whispered.

"You never actually told me," Lu said.

Jody was taken aback.

"You didn't want to talk about it," she said quickly. "Besides, all I really knew was that my family had a connection to the house. I didn't know the details until I called Lynda, like you told me to. What was I supposed to say? Oh, by the way, one of your ancestors killed one of mine and so my family put a curse on yours? That's crazy."

"And yet, apparently, it's exactly what happened," Lu said. "Look, I'm not angry. I know I avoided all of this, and I'm sure I didn't make it easy for you to tell me anything about the house or our history. It doesn't matter anyway. It was over a hundred years ago. Can we sleep now?"

"Yes, but we still have to tell her everything. Tomorrow," Jody said quietly.

"I can't tell her everything," Lu said. "I don't know everything. I don't know about the fire for one."

"Then tell her what you do know," Jody hissed.

They became silent for several minutes, each lost in her own thoughts.

"Lynda needs to come," Lu whispered.

Jody wasn't sure she heard correctly.

"What?"

"You heard me."

"Have Lynda come here? To this house?" Jody asked. She raised up on one elbow so she could look at Lu in the darkening room.

"There is more to this. I don't know everything, but Ruthie does. Maybe Lynda can actually talk to Ruthie," she said. "If so, she can tell us everything through Lynda instead of trying to use Anna."

Jody sat up fully and looked at Lu.

"Talk to Ruthie?" she asked. "Who are you?"

Lu laughed ruefully.

"It's the only answer," she said.

For Lu to suggest that Lynda try to talk to Ruthie was beyond the scope of anything Jody could have imagined. The events of the evening must have really affected Lu more than she realized.

"What changed your mind?" she asked.

"Anna is miserable. I owe it to her after all this time, to put my issues aside and help her. I didn't help her before, but I can help her now."

"You don't still feel guilty, do you? There's no reason to. You were protecting her," Jody said.

"I should have let it all come out long ago," Lu said. "I was too stubborn and wanted to control it all. I can't control it though. It's just too much and I don't understand any of it. I just want it over with. And I want to sleep now." She rolled over and pulled the blankets up to her ear.

Jody watched her for a moment and then pulled her own blankets to her chin as she settled back into the bed. She definitely understood Lu's feelings. She had her own guilt over things not said. She never told Lu about her jealousy towards Lynda and her abilities. It still stung, even after all this time, when she thought about the special relationship Lynda had with their mother. She felt ridiculous admitting to herself that she still had hurt feelings. She wished she could be the one to help Anna. She also wished she was generous enough to admit she couldn't and that she needed Lynda too.

She couldn't think of another way though. Lynda had the best chance to silence Ruthie so Anna could find peace. She didn't have to be psychic to know there was evil around them and they needed help. Something else was out there. Something bigger, and more dangerous, than Ruthie.

"I'll call her," she whispered to Lu's back.

"I already did," Lu replied. "She'll be here in the morning."

Chapter 25
2019

"Aunt Lynda!" Abhay said. "Come in. It's been so long. I'm glad you're here."

He opened the door wide and threw his arms around his aunt. She returned the hug with enthusiasm. She missed her nephew. This would be a good visit no matter what happened with Jody and Lu.

Jody hung back and watched them. Lynda looked healthy and happy. She was dressed in a long skirt and gauzy top that reached her fingertips. She made a racket when she moved from the dozen or so bracelets she wore. Her hair was grey and long down her back, much like May and Jody wore theirs. She wore no makeup. She didn't need it. Despite pushing sixty, Lynda was trim and strong. She smiled when she saw Jody. She held her arms open and they embraced. It had definitely been too long.

Lu stood back, watching the sisters. Lynda saw her hesitating.

"You too," Lynda said to her. "Get in here."

As the women hugged, the mood of the house lifted. What began as an awkward morning with very little conversation, turned into loud chatter as they talked over each other, trying to catch up as quickly as they could.

They sat on the couch in a row, alternately holding hands and then hugging, as though there had never been hurt feelings or anger. The years of tension and strain fell away.

"I wish May were here," Lynda said.

"Me too," Jody agreed. "But she wouldn't be comfortable with what's going on."

"That's an understatement," Abhay said. He was laughing at the thought of his mother talking to spirits.

Anna hugged Abhay.

"This feels great," she said.

"It does," Abhay agreed. "This is what we needed. It will be okay now."

The laughter and conversation continued nonstop for almost an hour. Finally, during a lull in the conversation, Anna jumped in.

"We have a space for you in the basement. It's really nice down there," she added quickly. "I know basements aren't exactly a happy place for this crowd."

Her efforts at levity were well received and everyone laughed gently.

"Thank you, dear," Lynda said as she stood. She took Anna's hands in hers and stared intently into her eyes.

"I understand you've had some interesting experiences."

Anna nodded. She wasn't sure what to say.

"Don't worry. I know the story and just by being here, I have a pretty good feeling for what's going on," Lynda said.

"Okay. Well please stay as long as you like," Anna said.

"Thank you, but I'm not sure I'm staying here," Lynda said. "In fact, depending on what happens, I'm not even sure you're staying."

Again, Anna was at a loss for words. She smiled awkwardly as the joking and teasing settled down. Good moods and laughter were quickly replaced with serious focus. Anna sat on the couch, beside Abhay, and watched Lynda.

She began to walk around the room, stopping periodically to look intently at Abhay and then at Anna. They attempted to ignore her stare and tried to carry on a casual conversation.

"I guess we're starting," Anna whispered to Abhay. "What do we do?"

Abhay shrugged. How was he supposed to know?

"So, what exactly did you two do when you worked together?" Abhay asked, nervously glancing towards Lynda and then back to Jody.

"When we were in college, we investigated hauntings all over the country. As you can probably see, Lynda is the medium and can actually talk to spirits. That's why we called her," Jody said.

"It's a family trait. You might even have the gift yourself," Lynda added. She paused for a second and looked thoughtfully at Abhay. Then she continued to move methodically around the room.

Abhay nodded, uncertain how to respond.

"Yes, this skill, gift, whatever you call it, has existed in our family for as long as I can remember," Jody continued. "In fact, it's been there for close to two hundred years. We have journals dating back to the mid 1800s kept by the witches in our family. That's how we found out about your house and, well, you know the rest."

"Then you've known about the curse for a long time?" Abhay asked.

"I knew someone in our family line had a connection to the house. I didn't know much more than that though, until Anna started talking about Ruthie. I called Lynda then and told her what was going on. We had our suspicions but no proof. Of course, when Lu and I got together, I let all of it go. It was hard to exist in both worlds. But Lynda continued to look into the stories. I only learned the details a few days ago," Jody said. She looked at Lynda. "You should tell the rest."

"Of course," Lynda said. She continued to pace as she talked.

"I assume everyone knows about William. He was a dangerous young man. He terrorized the small town and the young women who lived there. Then he made a mistake and killed the wrong young woman. That's where our families connect. The young woman was Lily's daughter. What's wrong?" she asked when everyone drew in their breath at once. "You already knew most of this, right?"

"Our daughter is named Lily," Abhay said.

Lynda smiled and then continued with her story.

"Old Lily was a witch. When the townspeople heard what she found in the cellar of that house, they turned into an angry mob. They stormed the house, found William and hung him from the tree that stands in front of the house. While this was going on, Lily hid nearby. She cast a curse just as William gasped for his last breath. His soul would never rest and would always be tied to the house," she said. She abruptly turned from the group and began to walk the edges of the room, muttering to herself.

"The house is haunted," Anna said. "I never really put it into words, but that explains so much. Aunt Lu, what do you think?"

"I agree. It explains a lot of the sounds and strange things that happened. I wish I hadn't been so stubborn," she said.

Lu turned to Jody.

"I'm sorry."

"It's okay," Jody said. "There were other issues to deal with at the time."

"Not unlike the other issues we have right now," Lynda interrupted quietly. When she had everyone's attention, she continued.

"Ruthie is here, but there's someone else, too." She looked

into the middle distance and her voice faded. Anna fought the urge to turn her head and see what Lynda was looking at.

"Who?" she asked as she rubbed her arms to make the goosebumps go away.

Something shifted in the air. Jody caught Lynda's eye and knew she felt it too.

"Do you know who Ruthie is?" Lynda asked. "And please don't say she's your imaginary friend. I think we're past that."

"I'm not sure," Anna began.

"Ruthie is William's little sister. She died in 1893, just before her seventh birthday. In your closet," she looked at Lu and Anna, "and alone. Isn't that right, Ruthie?"

Lynda's eyes swept upward. Everyone else looked up too. A filmy mist formed above their heads. It swirled just below the ceiling in large circles. Like a lazy tornado, a funnel slowly twisted itself down from the center. When it reached the floor, it began to take the shape of a little girl. The hazy apparition held an old doll.

Anna leaned forward and whispered, "Ruthie?"

The form shuddered and swept to the furthermost corner of the room. It floated there, its eyes wide and watching.

"I won't hurt you, I promise. None of us will," Lynda said gently. "Please talk to us."

"Ruthie?" Anna whispered again. Every cell of her body was awake. This was proof that everything she tried to ignore all those years was true. There really was another being that spoke to her. And protected her. She felt a combination of relief and disbelief at the same time as her mind tried to make sense of it all.

"I'm so sorry, Ruthie," Lynda continued. "It wasn't us. We would never hurt you. We didn't hurt William either. Please believe me. Yes, the curse came from our family, but it didn't come from any of us."

No one moved a muscle. Ruthie became a horizontal mist that drifted towards Lynda. The outline of her face formed close to Lynda's as the rest of her fluttered like a flag in a gentle breeze. Lynda held her own as the spirit sought to determine her sincerity. After a long minute, she seemed satisfied and Ruthie settled back into the hazy form of a little girl, still clutching her doll.

"Tell us your story, Ruthie," Lynda whispered and closed her eyes.

Anna and Abhay, Jody and Lu dared not move. No one was willing to risk upsetting the gentle balance created between the living and the dead.

"Ruthie says she lived with her Ma and Pa and her big brother William," Lynda began in a soft voice. "She says they were happy, but William was bad. He did bad things. She saw him kill a rabbit by skinning it alive. It made her sick. She heard Ma and Pa talking about other things too. He scared little children. He stole things. Oh no," Lynda added sadly. "Ruthie, I'm so sorry."

Lynda opened her eyes and looked at Anna.

"What? What did she say?" Anna asked.

"Ruthie says William hurt girls. Made them cry. She could hear them in the cellar. She's saying there was lots of blood, torn dresses, staring eyes, knives. I don't think she knows the words, but I think she's trying to say he tortured them. She says one of those girls was related to us. She said she's sorry too."

Anna grew quiet for a long time. She held her hand over her heart. Silent tears dripped down her chin. Was this what Ruthie protected her from? Was Ruthie afraid William would try to do that to her? Anna didn't have a chance to ask before Lynda spoke again.

"Ruthie says William hurt those girls like David hurt Anna and Lu."

"Maybe we should stop," Abhay said. He looked from Anna to Lu and back to Anna.

"No! Keep going," Anna said. "I'm okay. I want answers."

Lu nodded.

"Keep going," she urged.

"Ruthie says he never got in trouble because Pa would pay the families of the girls he hurt. And they made him promise not to go into town again. They even promised him a fancy new pocketknife if he behaved. And he did, for a while," Lynda said. Then she smiled.

"Oh, that sounds exciting. Tell me about that," she said. Lynda sat quietly for several seconds before she continued.

"Ruthie says, Ma and Pa were going to the World's Columbian Exhibition. All the way in Chicago. She wanted to go so bad, but she had to stay home with William. Before they left for the fair, Pa gave William that pocketknife he'd promised him. It was made from an antler and came from a company all the way in New York City. Ruthie was given a fancy doll," Lynda said. She became quiet again as she swayed gently from side to side. When she spoke, her voice was even quieter than before.

"I'm sorry you didn't get to go to the fair, Ruthie," Lynda whispered. "Why couldn't you go?"

"Her Ma wouldn't let her," Anna mumbled.

Lynda sat quietly for several seconds then nodded her head. She spoke slowly as she listened to Ruthie's story.

"Yes. Ruthie is happy that you remember that, Anna. She says Ma was always worried about her being sick and made her stay in a lot. That's why she couldn't go to the Exposition. Ma was afraid she would get sick and die like her other brother and sisters."

"So, they left her with William?" Anna interjected angrily.

Lynda held up a hand.

"William was a good brother, Ruthie says. He took care of her and was kind. The strange things he did were to hurt others, never her."

"Still..." Anna huffed. She felt herself wanting to protect Ruthie now. She'd always viewed Ruthie as older than her, as her protector. But now, seeing the little child she was, Anna felt more like her mother. Ruthie died at the same age as Lily is now.

Lynda continued.

"They had a big send off in town and they waved as the train pulled out with Ma and Pa. They walked back to the house, holding hands, talking. Ruthie says she was very happy. Then that night, William told Ruthie he was going to town. He told her to go to bed when it got dark, and he would be home by morning. Ruthie begged him to stay at the house with her, but he went out anyway. She wasn't scared. She wants us to know that," Lynda said to the group. "She really wants us to know that she was brave."

"I know," Anna said.

"Ruthie passed the time playing with her doll. She practiced writing and drew pictures in the dirt with a stick. She ate some bread with butter and a hunk of cheese. Then she went to bed. Ruthie says she woke up the next morning. There was a strange sound. She called for William."

Anna interjected.

"He was in the cellar."

"Ruthie says yes. When he came out, he had blood on him. He said it was from a cut but there was too much. While he was outside trying to wash it off, Ruthie snuck into the cellar," Lynda said. She looked around the room. She cleared her throat and took several sips of water. She rubbed her temples and stretched her neck from side to side.

"Is that it?" Abhay asked. "What was in the cellar?"

Lynda shook her head.

"I need a minute," she said. She cleared her throat again, took a long breath and then continued.

"Ruthie doesn't want to tell me what she saw. Instead, she's saying later that day a woman came. William was gone. The woman told Ruthie her name was Lily. She came by to check on Ruthie as a favor to her Ma. Ruthie let her in but panicked when the woman went straight to the cellar door. Ruthie tried to stop her. She told Lily that William didn't want anyone to go down there. Lily pushed Ruthie aside, pulled the door open and went down. Ruthie stayed upstairs worrying. She heard Lily scream. Then she ran out of the house without saying goodbye. Ruthie closed the cellar door and waited for William to come home."

"She says when he finally came home, he went straight to the cellar. She tried to ask him about what she saw, and she tried to tell him about the woman. He wouldn't listen to her. Instead he turned on her. His face was red, and he was angry. He told her to go to her room. He scared her, so she did what he said. She watched from her bedroom window and saw a crowd of people coming toward the house. They were angry and shouting. She heard William running up the stairs. He burst into her room, frantic. He made her sit in the closet. He told her she would be safe there and told her he would be back soon. Ruthie sat in the closet and hugged her doll. William closed the door. He moved something heavy in front of the door so they couldn't find her."

"Oh, no," Anna sobbed. "Oh Ruthie!"

"She said it was dark in there. Ruthie says she was brave. She heard shouting and crashes in the house. Women were screaming. Men were cursing. Then it got very quiet. She fell asleep. When she woke up, she was hungry. She pushed on the door as hard as she could, but she couldn't move it. She called for William, but he never came. Ruthie said she was lonely for a while, but eventually she fell asleep forever."

"The scratches in the closet," Lu whispered.

"Ruthie says she woke up when Ma and Pa got home. Ma was crying and even Pa cried. Ruthie said they put her in a box and buried her. She was confused because she was still there, but they couldn't see her. She saw them put William in a box. He was still there too. She found him swinging from the tree in front of the house. She thought he was playing, and she wanted to play too. But, Ruthie says, William was different. He was mean and scary. Ruthie stayed in her room, close to her doll, and away from William. She says one day, Ma put her doll in a box too. She put it in the attic and cried a lot. Ruthie says she stayed there, hiding from William and from everyone else too. Lu, she says she came out when you were born. She liked you and tried to talk to you when you were older."

"I remember," Lu said. "She tried to get my attention. I'm sorry."

"She knows Lu. It's okay. And Jody, Abhay, she said she's not mad at us. She realizes now it wasn't our fault."

The misty form swirled around the room once and then disappeared.

Ruthie, are you here? Anna thought. There was no answer. Anna wasn't sure how she felt about that. She surprised herself when her next thought was, *I miss you.*

Lynda blew her nose loudly, bringing Anna's thoughts back to what they'd just witnessed. No longer a room of doubters, they each had much to think about. They looked at each other, uncertain what to do. They looked to Lynda for guidance.

Lynda swallowed the rest of her water and stood to stretch.

"Well, I guess that's it for now anyway," she said.

"Wait! I have so many questions," Anna said.

"Who else was here?" Abhay asked.

"Are you kidding me?" Lu said.

Lynda smiled gently.

"We'll get our answers soon," she said. "But it's not on our timetable, I'm afraid. Ruthie is still a little girl. She'll talk when she's ready."

Suddenly, Anna stood. She turned on her heel and marched out of the room.

Abhay looked at Lu and Jody then watched his wife walk away. Almost immediately they heard grunting sounds.

"Hold on," he said as he stood. He followed Anna and found her in the hallway. She was jumping, trying to reach the pull on the attic door, and missing every time.

"What are you doing?" he asked. He put a hand on her shoulder and reached above her for the cord. He pulled the attic ladder down and Anna immediately scrambled up it.

"Hold on," she said as she reached the top of the ladder. The insulation in the attic made her itch. She rubbed her nose and scratched her neck as she looked around, anxious to find what she was looking for and get out of there as quickly as she could.

Finally, she found what she needed. A small box, lovingly taped and labeled with the handwriting of a child. She ripped the box open and pulled out the doll. Clutching it to her chest, she dropped to her knees and rocked back and forth.

Abhay had made his way up the ladder and now stood beside her.

"I remember," Anna whispered.

"Come on," he said, helping her stand.

He guided her back down the ladder as she clutched the doll with one hand and the ladder with the other.

Lu and Jody stood at the bottom of the ladder. When Lu saw what Anna carried, she cried out.

"That's Ruthie!"

"I forgot all about that doll," Jody added. "We packed her away when we moved, but obviously we never unpacked her. Why didn't you say something?" she asked Anna.

"I don't know," Anna said. "I guess I forgot about her. I remember finding her though."

Chapter 26
1982

Anna scrambled to the furthest corner of the attic and pulled her knees to her chest. Daddy was all angry about something again. He started to go after the dog, but it was smart and ran off. Anna, however, wasn't so lucky. He got her a few times real good, before she squirmed from his grasp and ran. She sprinted up the stairs to her bedroom but decided in an instant to keep going up one more flight. It was unlikely he would climb to her room. He had only made the effort a few times and Anna swore she wouldn't make the mistake of being there if he should decide to come again. Neither Mama nor Daddy would climb the stairs all the way to the attic, she was sure of that.

She pressed her back against the rough wood and took a deep breath. Her arm and back ached from where Daddy had gotten in a few licks. She pushed her short sleeve up and looked at the red spot that would soon turn shades of black, blue and eventually green and yellow. She twisted her body to see the four matching spots on the back of her arm when she noticed something. It looked like a tiny hand.

Heart in her throat, she scooted closer. She peered between two heavier boxes. It was a hand, and it was dangling from another box that was shoved far back in the attic. She reached in as far as she could, but she couldn't quite get her fingers to it. She shifted her body and put her feet on one of the boxes. Then she braced her back against the other and pushed. Finally, the boxes moved so she could reach the smaller box. Anna sneezed.

The box was covered in dust. A ribbon was loosely tied around it, keeping the lid on despite the small hand that managed to escape. She wondered why she hadn't noticed it before. Anna slowly and carefully pulled off the ribbon. Something was written on the lid. She ran her hand gently over the top to clear the dust. The name "Ruthie" was written in fancy script. She set the lid aside. The small hand had escaped from a yellowed blanket. Anna pulled the edges of the blanket out. She tucked the arm back into the box, next to the doll's body.

She sat back and looked at the doll. She was really old. Her blonde hair stood out at all angles and a small bow clung on perilously to the end of a matted strand. Her left leg was twisted so her toes pointed in, and she was missing a shoe. Her pale yellow, eyelet lace dress looked very old fashioned. Anna loved her immediately.

"Hi there, Ruthie," she said.

Ruthie was Anna's greatest treasure and would need a safe place to stay. Anna tried to hide her in her closet with her other special things, but Ruthie hated being in there. She refused to go in and would make a huge fuss if Anna even mentioned it. It was decided that when Anna wasn't around, Ruthie would hide under her bed. It was unlikely Mama or Daddy would climb the stairs to get to her room, and it was even more unlikely they would get on their knees to look under her bed. Ruthie would be safe there.

Chapter 27
2019

"Oh! That's the same doll," Lynda exclaimed when she saw Anna.

Anna told them how she found the doll in the attic when she was a child.

"She must have been up there all those years. How sad," she murmured. "That poor mother."

"Poor Ruthie," Lu added.

"Have you heard from her?" Lynda asked Anna.

"No. I tried but no answer," she said.

"Did she always talk back to you. Before?" Lynda asked.

Anna nodded her head and sat down.

"It's strange," she said. "I feel weird, alone. She's not guiding me."

As each one found a comfortable place to sit, Abhay and Jody brought out a water pitcher and coffee pot. They poured their drinks, then one by one looked at Lynda.

Lynda slowly stirred creamer into her coffee, ignoring the watchful gaze of those in the room.

Finally, she lifted her head.

"I feel her," Lynda said. "She's back."

Everyone sat silently and waited. No one knew what they were waiting for. It had already been an emotional day with many questions answered by Ruthie herself. Still the tension increased, and the air felt thick and heavy. Moments passed as they looked at each other, at the ceiling and at the floor. Anna wondered if Ruthie would show herself again.

She jumped when every mug and glass on the coffee table shattered. The word *Run* flashed through her mind. It was quickly followed by the word *Fire*.

Everyone moved at once to wipe up the mess except Anna and Lynda. Anna tried to calm her racing heart. She spoke out loud.

"Ruthie! No! It's okay. We are safe now, we don't have to run."

Abhay stopped cleaning up the mess. He sat back down next to Anna and ignored the slow drip of coffee on the carpet. Lu and Jody did the same. Now they all squinted and strained to catch the wispy tendrils floating through the air that signaled Ruthie was there.

"I'm not strong enough!" Ruthie's voice rang through Lynda.

"I am," Anna said. "We all are."

Her confidence faded as Abhay grabbed her hand. He was slumping over and slowly tumbled to the floor.

"Can't breathe," he gasped.

Anna dropped to his side.

"Abhay, what is it?" She turned his face towards her so she could see his eyes.

"Look at me," she demanded.

Abhay put his hands on Anna's shoulders and shoved. Anna flew back and landed on her bottom. Stunned, she scrambled back to her feet, ready to fight. Then she froze.

Another form was hovering over Abhay. It looked like Ruthie did, hazy and unformed. But it wasn't Ruthie. It was

William. He was covered in blood and a thick rope was draped around his neck. Anna shrieked as the end of the rope touched Abhay's face.

When the rope touched him, Abhay sprang into action. He pulled himself to his feet and stood with his legs spread wide, fists at his side.

The apparition of the boy changed too. He stood in front of Abhay, his hazy figure, menacing and threatening as he lifted a finger and pointed it at Abhay.

"You stole my knife," he said in a surprisingly strong voice.

"So?" Abhay challenged.

Anna was shocked. She couldn't believe Abhay was reacting this way. She started to say something, but Ruthie hushed her with a command to be quiet. Anna was relieved to hear Ruthie again.

Help him, Ruthie.

"Don't protect the witch!" William snapped. He looked at Anna and grinned. Anna's stomach dropped. That evil smile was familiar. She took a single step back. Then William turned back to Abhay.

Abhay stood tall and steady for a man who didn't believe in ghosts a mere twenty-four hours ago. He adapted quickly and refused to back down in the face of this fearsome sight. His fists were still clenched at his side, and Anna wondered if he would try to punch the spirit. Then she wondered if that was even possible. She shook her head as more random thoughts passed through her mind. She had to focus.

It helped when Lynda suddenly bellowed, "William Marshall! You stop this now! You are not welcome here! Go away!"

He turned slowly. His intense gaze shifted to Lynda.

"No, it's you," he said. "And, you. I remember you," he pointed to Jody. "You are the witches who cursed me. It was your daughter I had in the cellar," he smiled that cruel smile

178

again. Anna remembered why it was familiar. It reminded her of David, her father.

Like an old movie made from stills spliced together, William jerked and moved towards them. He would disappear and then immediately reappear each time a little closer. In no time, he crossed the room, leaving Abhay to watch helpless and flustered, as William moved closer and closer to his aunts.

William's arms were out in front of him, his hands grasping at the air. Jody and Lynda were rooted to their spots. Jody out of fear, Lynda out of anger.

Just as William was about to reach Jody, a rush of cold air blasted through the room. It picked William up and slammed him into the wall.

Lynda quickly gathered her family behind her, Jody and Abhay instinctively moved to her side. Anna tried to pull her husband and aunt back. This was her battle after all. But the three wouldn't budge.

"Stop this now!" Lynda's voice boomed.

Icy cold air continued to swirl through the room and the hazy form of William began to shift and take shape again as it drifted down from the wall. The air was oppressive and dense. It was hard to breathe.

Ruthie's tiny six-year-old form emerged from the mist. She faced the ghost of her brother without hesitation or fear.

"Move," William bellowed.

"No," Ruthie said. "I won't let you hurt them."

"I can make him hurt them," William said, pointing his finger at Abhay. "Like I did David and the ones before him."

Anna's stomach lurched as images flooded her mind. That sick smile. It brought everything back in a rush of emotion. She remembered why she was in the hospital all those years ago. She remembered that night in her room. She remembered all the beatings, and she remembered exactly how she got bruises. She remembered David's thin smile. Anna felt Lu's hand grasp hers. She knew Lu was remembering too.

Ruthie had always protected Anna's mind even if she couldn't protect her body. She kept the evil at bay as best she could. Now she needed Anna's help as she faced her brother's fury and tried to protect her one more time.

Anna looked at Lu.

"Come on," she said.

They ran to the back door, each reading the other's mind, and still holding hands.

"I'll get it," Anna said, raising her voice. The cacophony in the room was intense. Vases and picture frames were falling from shelves, the TV tipped over and shattered, books thudded to the floor. It felt like a tornado was ripping through her home.

She flung the door open and stepped outside. The sudden silence of the yard threw her off balance. Her head felt heavy and her ears were ringing as she stumbled to the chair where Aunt Jody had put the carving she took from Abhay.

Anna unwrapped it quickly and touched the wood. She was prepared for it to burn her like it burned Aunt Jody, but she didn't feel anything. She grabbed it and ran back to the house.

Lu held the door open when she saw Anna coming. Anna entered the house, holding the carving high for all to see.

"William!" she yelled.

Suddenly everything stopped. The whirlwind died down. William and Ruthie stopped fighting.

"That's mine," William said. He began to move towards Anna.

"Burn it," Jody said under her breath.

Anna looked at Lynda. She nodded once.

"Now," she said.

Anna quickly placed the carving on the hearth of the fireplace. She scooted it back a little and then looked frantically for a lighter. As if on cue, one fell from the mantle into her hand. Ruthie knocked it over.

This won't work, Anna thought. She flicked the lighter a few times before she had a steady flame. She could see William just beyond her peripheral vision. He was getting closer. Her hands shook as she moved the flame to the carving. Immediately it went out. She fumbled with the lighter again as she felt William's intimidating form hovering above her head.

"Hey, asshole," Abhay called. "Want this?" He held the pocketknife in the air and waved it around.

"That's mine," William said. He swirled in place and began to move back towards Abhay.

"Anna?" Abhay said as calmly as he could while he watched William's approach.

"Hurry," Jody said.

The more Anna tried to hurry, the more she fumbled with the lighter. She sensed William growing stronger. His malevolent presence was filling the room. The wispy edges of his form became more solid each moment that passed.

Hurry, Ruthie urged Anna. *I know you can do this.*

Anna took a deep breath and made her mind calm down. She flicked the lighter one more time and cheered when she managed a steady flame. She pulled the carving back out of the fireplace and held it aloft with one hand. With the other hand, she moved the flame to the edge of it. The carving exploded in a burst of white light and then disappeared. Anna jumped back, surprised but not hurt. The room was eerily silent.

"Is he gone?" Anna asked. She looked at her fingers and hand. No burns at all.

"Yes," Lynda said.

"Really? That worked?" Abhay asked.

"Don't question it," Jody said. "Just be happy it's over."

Anna sighed and melted into Abhay's arms. Lu and Jody pulled Lynda close. The small group embraced each other in silence as their adrenaline subsided and pounding hearts calmed.

The quiet was interrupted by Abhay.

"What do I do with this?" He held the pocketknife in the palm of his hand.

"Keep it," Lynda said simply.

Anna looked around the room.

"Ruthie?"

Ruthie was gone.

Chapter 28
2019

L u and Anna walked through the park. It was a glorious day with a cool breeze and bright sun. Lily was back at home happily being spoiled by Jody and Lynda. She was thrilled to have discovered yet another great aunt who would ruin her. Abhay had been spoiling her as well. He said he owed it to her for how he acted.

"I really don't think she thought anything of it," Anna had told him that morning before she and Lu left.

"I do though," he said.

While she and Lu walked and talked, Lily was busy making ice cream sundaes while three adults catered to her every whim.

"She's going to be a monster when we get back," Anna said to Lu.

"Reminds me of someone else I know," Lu said.

"I wasn't that bad," Anna exclaimed.

Lu sat down on a nearby bench and sighed. She stretched her legs out in front of her.

"Feeling your age?" Anna asked. Lu was in her sixties, still strong and healthy like her sisters, but Anna noticed sometimes she moved a little slower.

"Yup," she said. She rubbed her left knee. "You know I'm teasing you about being spoiled. After everything you went through, it's amazing you turned out as well as you did. I am so proud of you, you know that, right?"

"If I turned out okay, it's only because of you and Jody."

"You remember everything now?" Lu asked carefully.

Anna nodded.

"I think so," she said. "Most of it."

"Jody was right. I should have let her talk all those years ago and let her tell you what she knew. I'm sorry. I feel responsible for everything. If only I had told you what happened to me, especially when I knew it was happening to you too. I tried, but..." Lu choked back a sob.

"Aunt Lu," Anna said. She put her hand on Lu's arm.

"There is nothing for you to apologize for. Even if William was affecting the men in our house, they still had a choice. They chose how they acted. Abhay proved that when he made the right choice. He fought William and won before he even knew who William was. David could have done the same. Grandfather could have done the same. They chose to hurt you and me. They are the ones who should be sorry."

"But if I had told you, maybe you could have remembered more. Maybe you wouldn't have needed Ruthie so badly. You would have been more confident."

"Maybe," Anna said. "Maybe not."

They sat in silence, each thinking her own thoughts and remembering her own past. Lu felt guilty for hiding the truth from Anna for so long, but Anna was grappling with her own guilt as well. She was almost certain she started the fire that killed her parents. The only hope she had was that it was an accident.

Finally, she broke the silence. "I still don't remember the night of the fire. I don't know, maybe I did start it. Considering all that happened, I would have had a reason."

184

Suddenly Lu sat up straight and looked at Anna.

"Ruthie did it!" she said.

"What? Ruthie did what?" Anna asked.

"The fire. She started it. Think about it. Ruthie knocked things over when she was angry or sad. She knocked things over to distract the adults in the house. She protected both of us by making a noise the only way she could. Even last night, Ruthie broke the glasses right before William showed up. It's like she was trying to warn us. Ruthie did it to protect you," Lu said.

"You think Ruthie knocked something over and that started the fire?" Anna asked. She was having a difficult time believing it was that simple.

"Yup, that's it. Case closed, Ruthie did it. She knocked over something flammable, and it caught the bed on fire. It makes perfect sense." She sat back, satisfied.

Anna wasn't so sure it could be wrapped up that easily, and she still felt uncomfortable with the memory gap. But Lu looked so relieved and so confident in her assessment, Anna decided to go along with it. She was right, it did make sense in a strange way.

"I still wish I could remember more," Anna said.

"You might never, honey. But I think you can rest easy knowing you aren't responsible," Lu said.

Anna stood and helped Lu to her feet.

"Let's go home and deprogram my daughter," she said.

"Lily, do you want this doll?" Anna yelled through the house. She wasn't sure where Lily was. The ice cream party was over. Lu, Jody, and Lynda had left in a flurry of hugs and kisses with promises to get together again and soon.

Abhay had cleaned up the broken glass before Lily got

home that morning and now, he was working his magic trying to get coffee stains out of the carpet.

Anna found the doll sitting where she had left her on the couch. She thought about putting her back in her box, in the attic, but she felt guilty. The doll represented Ruthie, and Ruthie was special. She didn't deserve to be stuffed into a box and tucked away.

"What?" Lily asked as she bounded into the room. She still had an ice cream mustache that matched the stains on her shirt.

Anna smiled.

"You're a mess," she said, pulling Lily toward her.

She used mom spit to clean Lily's face with her thumb as Lily squirmed and pulled away.

"Ewwww, gross," she said. She started to run off, but Anna stopped her.

"Hey! Do you want this doll?" she asked again.

Lily looked at the doll, sitting on the couch. She was really old and weird looking. Her hair was a mess and her leg was broken. Her face was creepy too. It had tiny lines all over it. Lily screwed up her face.

"You could keep her on a shelf in your room," Anna suggested.

Lily paused for a moment, appearing to deeply consider her mother's idea.

"No, thank you," she said primly. Then she turned and skipped from the room.

"Well, back in the box for you, I guess," Anna said.

"Probably for the best," Abhay added. "Hold on."

He disappeared for a moment while Anna smoothed the doll's dress and tried to tame her hair. When he returned, Abhay handed her a small box and a roll of packing tape.

Anna laid the doll in the box. She arranged her dress carefully. She smoothed her hair and fixed the bow. Then she tucked the doll's arms in.

186

Abhay leaned over her and placed the pocketknife in the box next to the doll. He kissed Anna's cheek.

"Thank you, Ruthie," Anna murmured.

Then she closed the lid and sealed it shut.

Chapter 29
2019

"Are you absolutely sure?" Abhay asked again. "I can do this on my own. You don't have to come."

"I'm sure," Anna said.

"Come on, Daddy," Lily pulled Abhay towards the car.

Anna opened the door, and Lily climbed into the backseat. She buckled herself into her booster seat. Anna handed her an iPad so she could watch movies as they drove.

"I really am okay," she said as she opened her door. "Let's go."

The drive to Jonesboro took the usual hour and half. They had to stop twice for Lily to use the bathroom. Abhay joked that he drove there and back one day and didn't have to stop once.

"You're a boy," Lily informed him as though that made all the difference. She had put the iPad away now and was excited to see where her Mommy was born.

Anna thought she was prepared to see the house again and it wouldn't affect her. But as soon as they pulled off the paved road, she felt a wave of nausea. The sound of gravel crunching paired with the car lurching in and out of ruts and holes threatened to make her vomit.

"Oof," she said, putting one hand on her stomach and the other over her mouth.

"You okay?" Abhay asked quickly.

"Yes, just nerves," she said.

They followed the bumpy road around the curve and the house came into view.

"There it is, Lily," Anna said. "The house where Aunt Lu and I grew up."

"Wow," Lily said.

They parked in front of the house, next to the old tree that never grew. She wondered if this was the tree William was hung from. She shivered despite the heat and shook off the feeling. She was determined that this trip would be a positive experience. They were selling the house and the land. Anna wanted to be involved in every step of the process. It would serve as closure for her.

"Lily, come with me," Abhay called. "We're going out back. There's an old car back there I want to check out."

"Don't let Lily climb around it," Anna called back. "There might be snakes. And it's rusty. It's been there since I was a kid."

Abhay waved his hand at Anna as Lily bounced through the tall grass towards him. Anna watched them walk off, holding hands, until she couldn't see them any longer.

She made her way around the perimeter of the house to the part that was still standing. She paused to get her bearings. The kitchen was here, in front of her. Only one end of it was damaged. Next to it would have been her parents' bedroom. Anna walked a little farther and peered into the hollowed-out shell of the house. She wanted to see the kitchen.

Careful not to step on burned or rotten floorboards, she slowly picked her way through the wreckage and found the part of the kitchen that still stood.

She looked at the row of cabinets and remembered climbing on top of the counter to look for food in them, terrified she would be caught and get in trouble. She gingerly opened one. Its hinges squealed and she jumped. She instinctively froze, and then steadied herself, one hand on the counter and one over her heart. She laughed.

"No more ends of the loaf for me," she said. Her voice sounded hollow in the empty house.

Next, she turned to the refrigerator. The front of it had been removed, and it was empty now. Anna could still picture a row of beer cans on the top shelf and the little drawer where Amber kept the cheese. She looked at the sink wondering if water still ran. When she turned the faucet the old pipes rumbled, but no water came out.

Finished with the kitchen, Anna wanted to make her way further into the house. She would have loved to go upstairs to her old room but knew the structure would be dangerously unstable. She acknowledged that she probably shouldn't even be on the first floor, so she promised herself she would be super careful. She made her way down the hallway, cautiously testing each step before putting her full weight down. Soon she stood at the doorway to what used to be her parents' bedroom.

She braced herself for what she knew would be a shock. Uncertain what she thought she would find, she carefully peered into the room. Sunlight streamed in where the roof had burned away. A large chunk of the outside wall was gone, the remains crumbling. The room was completely empty except for the dust motes that fluttered around.

"What did you think you'd find?" Anna asked ruefully as she rubbed her itchy nose. Her allergies were going wild. There was nothing here. She might as well leave. As she turned, her vision suddenly narrowed. Blackness surrounded her except for a small circle of light and even that was hazy. She steadied herself with one hand on the wall, staring at the floor. She was dizzy and disoriented.

Her first thought was that she was having another panic attack. That didn't seem right though. This felt different. She blinked several times and rubbed her eyes. Fresh air would help. She would leave.

She opened her eyes and was relieved that her vision had returned to normal. As she surveyed the room one more time, she saw something move from the corner of her eye. Whipping her head around, she was startled to see a little girl standing in the doorway with a doll under her arm. She carried a glass in one hand and a sandwich in the other.

"Ruthie!" Anna exclaimed. It had been almost a month since she heard from her old friend, and she was missing her.

Anna watched the little girl move into the room. As she walked, the room changed. It began to look like it did that night so many years ago. Soon the bed stood in front of her. The TV on the dresser materialized against the far wall. There were even dirty clothes on the floor.

And the little girl was definitely not Ruthie.

Anna knew her mind was playing tricks on her. She rubbed her eyes again.

"That's it," she muttered. "I'm out of here."

As she turned to leave, she heard the little girl speak.

"Shouldn't smoke in bed," she said. "You might start a fire."

When Anna looked back, the girl was standing next to the bed. David's sleeping form had materialized as well. He had a lit cigarette in the hand that rested on his chest. A Mason jar of clear liquid was tucked beside him. Anna watched as the little girl reached over his chest. She hooked a single finger over the lip of the jar. It tipped and liquid flowed across the mattress. Then she poked the man's hand. It dropped to his side.

"You had a choice," she said. Then she walked out of the room.

Anna stood rooted to the spot. She watched a bright red ember fall off the end of the cigarette. She heard a whoosh as the mattress ignited. Blue flame spread across the room.

She jumped when she heard a single word. It came from the kitchen.

"Why?"

Anna waited. She knew the girl would be coming down the hallway any second now with her doll and her sandwich.

When she passed, Anna followed her. They walked down the front hall where Lori had died. Anna paused there. She brushed away a tear. The little girl kept walking, through the front door, across the porch, and down the steps. Then she sat down, crisscross applesauce in the yard. She ate her sandwich and gently rocked her doll in her arms. Anna watched from the porch as the little girl faded away.

From where she stood, Anna could see most of the front yard and the tree line beyond. She smelled honeysuckle and turned her face towards the breeze. It was finally peaceful here. She walked to the tree that stood in the front yard. She hadn't noticed the blossoms on it when they pulled in. She smiled as she reached up and picked a pink one. She would give it to Lily.

Her cat is possessed. She sees murders in her dreams. She might be married to a serial killer... Grab your copy of Silent Screams today!

If you enjoyed this book, please consider leaving a review. It helps others decide if they might enjoy the book, and it's one of the best ways to support indie authors.

I'd love to stay in touch! Join my newsletter for sneak peeks, deals and other specials for subscribers only.

Fat Cat Publishing

Scan the QR code to join our newsletter!

Paranormal Women's Fiction
   Extra-Ordinary Midlife by Lynn M. Stout

Dystopian Crime Thriller
   Paranoia by B.E. Stout

Paranormal Domestic Thriller
   Not Safe at Home by May Black

Ingram Content Group UK Ltd.
Milton Keynes UK
UKHW011014300323
419408UK00001B/211